Suspended Entrapment

THE PAST LIFE PRISM SERIES TIME TRAVEL SUSPENSE
BOOK THREE

JULIE BAWDEN DAVIS

Roses
ARE
RED
PUBLISHING

Cover by Judy Bullard (customebookcovers.com)

Book design by Julie Bawden-Davis

Prism logo design by Kery Bailey

Roses are Red logo design by Kyle Kane

This is a work of fiction. Characters and incidents are the product of the author's imagination. Any perceived likenesses are coincidental.

ISBN-978-1-955265-27-0

ISBN-1-955265-27-5

Distributed by Roses Are Red Publishing

rosesareredpublishing.com

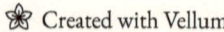 Created with Vellum

Acknowledgments

As they say, it takes a village. Here's my village. I'm supremely grateful to each of these fabulous people!

ARC Reading Gems
Kery Bailey
Julie Schlueter
Susa Fraccaroli
Trish Darrenkamp
Marilyn Smith
Lisa Starkey
Beth Helm
Chelle Young
Jacquelyn Gray
Ellen Ocean
Heather Wamboldt
MelK
Amber Mancebo
Pros
Judy Bullard, cover design
Kyle Kane, Roses are Red logo design
Kery Bailey, Prism logo design
Sabrina Wildermuth, design consultation

To those with whom we learn lesson upon lesson.

I n the dark, moonless night, the Mercedes Benz crawled toward her. Fear seized Suzette, and she struggled to breathe. She glanced back to see that he stood next to the closed shop out of sight from the street. He gave her a curt nod toward the car.

She knew from what she'd heard and seen with the other girls that she had to do what she was told. If she didn't, she would suffer. Vincent had been so nice when they met, telling her he loved her and giving her gifts. But when she moved into the house, he made it clear that he owned her.

Suzette pulled the front of her blouse down and sashayed to the Benz, prepared to convince the occupant he wanted a date.

The man reached over from the driver's side and pushed the passenger door open. "How much?" he asked.

Suzette thought about the speech she'd been forced to memorize, then sputtered, "It depends on what you want."

Vincent's presence from the shadows pushed her nearer the man's car. "If it's a full, then twenty, and partial, fifteen," she said.

"That's a lot of money."

Hysteria lodged in Suzette's throat as she struggled to find her voice. Finally, she said, "That's the price, sir."

He eyed her, then replied, "You called me sir. I like that you have some manners. Hurry up and get in."

Suzette teetered on the peep-toe heels one of the girls had lent her and got into the car. She looked at the man, whose eyes had a funny sheen to them now. She wanted more than anything to get out and run but knew there was no point. Vincent would catch her.

The man reached under his seat and handed her a flask. "Drink some of this."

Hands shaking, Suzette turned the cap, then took a drink and held back a cough as whiskey made a corrosive path to her belly.

"More," he ordered.

She took another mouthful. Though the alcohol burned her throat, she had begun to feel hazy. Maybe this wouldn't be so bad after all.

Chapter 1 - Present Day

Sophia pulled her bedroom blinds open and gazed out at the early morning. The forecast had promised rain today, but she could see the sun peeking out. She pulled her phone out of the charger and powered it on, greeted by a text message from her grandmother three hours earlier. *Boarding my flight at Athens International! Can't wait to see you both.*

Sophia smiled, excitement washing through her at soon seeing her grandmother. She went into the kitchen to brew some coffee, surprised to find there was already some made. Had she forgotten to empty it last night? She touched the side of the pot. Still slightly warm.

"Teddy?" she cried out. "You up?"

She walked back down the hallway and knocked softly on his door. "Teddy?"

No answer, but she heard something fall. Alarmed, she opened the door to find him slumped over on his desk, a book upside down on the floor. She walked in quietly to stand over her son, whose shoulders softly rose and fell, a nearly full cup of coffee on the desk beside him. She touched him lightly on the shoulder, and he bolted up, his eyes wide.

"Mom, what time is it?"

"It's still early. You're not late for school, if that's what you're worried about. Did you study all night?"

Teddy ran his hands through his hair, then retrieved the book from the floor. "Just about all night. I have to pass the trig test today."

Sophia reached for the cup of coffee. "How about I heat this in the microwave for you?"

Teddy raised his eyebrows. "No lecture about how staying up was counterproductive?"

Sophia laughed. "That lecture obviously didn't stick, so why bother. Want me to make you some eggs?"

Teddy gave her a grateful look as he stood. "Yes, thank you. I'm going to jump in the shower first if that's okay."

"I'd recommend it," said Sophia.

"Are you saying I smell?" He grinned as he took fresh clothing out of his bureau.

"I'm pleading the fifth," said Sophia, turning to leave the room. "Reminder that your grandmother comes in tonight."

"I might forget how to do the quadratic formula on today's exam, but I would never forget that grandma is coming in tonight," said Teddy. "Cerise can't wait to meet her."

As Sophia walked back into the kitchen, her phone pinged to show a calendar reminder of an appointment with her new past life client, Lorraine Donavan, later that morning.

Sophia broke several eggs into a bowl, then whisked them quickly and turned on the stove. After dicing up ham and cheese, she threw everything into the hot skillet.

When she set two plates of eggs on the kitchen island a couple of minutes later, a shadowy form suddenly appeared a few feet in front of her. "Phillip," she gasped. Though Sophia should be used to his comings and goings by now, it still shook her when he appeared all of a sudden. She put her hands on the island to steady herself.

"Hello, my love," he said. "About your grandmother's visit."

"Yes?" she said, suddenly anxious. "Is Grandmother going to be okay on her flight?"

"Yes, yes, it's nothing like that."

Sophia relaxed. "Then what is it?"

"Her visit will be significant for all of you," he said.

Sophia stood up straighter. "Significant, how?" She heard a sound in the hallway. Teddy coming.

"Significant how?" she asked again.

"That's all I can tell you," said Phillip before vanishing.

Teddy ambled into the room. "Did you say something?"

"Just talking to myself about work."

He sat down and picked up his fork. "This looks great, thanks."

Sophia took a sip of coffee. "Your exam sounds pretty important."

Teddy shoveled eggs into his mouth and replied between bites, "It's the first big exam since school started and worth a third of my grade. I know I'm already accepted to Chapman next year, but the last thing I want to do is take summer school to pass trig."

"I doubt that will happen," said Sophia.

"I dunno. I'm not all that great at math. Was dad?"

"Your father was a math whiz," she said. "I'm afraid that you got your problems with math from me. Definitely not my best subject. You've probably noticed I never offer to help you."

"I kinda figured that was the case when I asked you what an integer was a few years ago, and you had to look it up. What else was dad good at in school?"

"The question would probably be what he wasn't good at," said Sophia.

"Do you think I'll have any professors that knew him at Chapman?"

Sophia thought for a moment. "It's possible."

Teddy smiled. "I'd really like that."

Sophia's heart hitched at the hope in her son's voice. "At the very least, you'll be walking the same halls your father walked."

"I thought about that when I accepted their offer to attend," said Teddy.

Sophia was surprised. "You did?"

"Yeah, it wasn't something I consciously thought of, but it was at the back of my mind, you know." He ate the last of his eggs and took a swallow of coffee and stood. "I gotta go. I'll see you tonight for the trip to the airport. Is it okay if Cerise goes?"

"Sure, of course. I'll get your dishes. Good luck with your exam."

Teddy grabbed his backpack and called over his shoulder as he headed to the front door, "Thanks, I'm going to need it."

When the door banged shut, Sophia looked at the chair where Teddy had been seated, half expecting to see Phillip reappear, but there was no one there. She finished her coffee, the silence in the condo now seeming to echo.

"Sitting by the window won't bring him back, little love."

Sophia wiped the tears from her cheeks with her fingers, angry at herself for how they kept coming. Her grandmother had been with her since the news of Phillip's death in Afghanistan a month before, and she was still crying throughout the days. She looked at her through hazy tears. "I thought you said I should take as long as I need to mourn Phillip. Are you suggesting I stop?"

Her grandmother held a cup of tea in her hands, the scent of chamomile wafting toward Sophia. She set the cup on the end table next to her, then motioned for Sophia to scoot over on the love seat so she could join her. Setting her hand lightly on her granddaughter's knee, she said in a quiet voice, "Mourn as long as you need to mourn, but you and I both know that you're doing more than that." Her grandmother paused for a moment, then resumed. "Having this ability to sense those who have passed as we do is a gift and a curse all at the same time." She sighed. "When your Grandfather Nico left me, I could sense him near me day and night. I sat on our balcony in Greece and stared out at the sea, and I could feel him next to me. While that is comforting in its own way, in another way you don't want to get stuck there, if that makes sense."

Sophia pushed stray, tear-soaked hairs from her face and nodded. "It does. So, you had the same experience with Grandpa Nico? Knowing he was with you, yet he had left you. It's so exasperating and sad all at the same time. How long did it take you to get over it?" As soon as Sophia uttered the words, she knew her grandmother's answer.

"You never get over it, but you do get past the sadness and move on. At some point, you develop a sort of long-distance relationship with the person. But before that occurs, you must face the fact that you have lost the physical, earthbound experience with them. That is something you must mourn, and doing so takes time."

Her grandmother reached for the tea and gently placed it in Sophia's hands. "Drink, it will help settle and center you. And then I am going to make you something to eat. You need to keep the baby nourished."

As Sophia sipped her tea, and her grandmother rubbed her back, she felt fresh tears spring to her eyes. This time, not because of Phillip, but because of the overwhelming gratitude she felt for her grandmother's presence. Setting the cup in her lap, she choked out, "Thank you for everything. I don't think I could have gotten through this without you."

Her grandmother took the cup and held it for her. "I have no doubt that you could have gotten through this without me. But I'm glad I can be here for you. In person, in the flesh." She enveloped Sophia in her arms as a new torrent of tears came.

As she waited for Lorraine, who was late for their appointment, Sophia recalled their first session. She had ruled out the woman having other psychological problems, determining her issue just a past life situation. She smiled at the word *just*. Past lives, she'd been finding, could have a major role in current life situations.

Sophia opened her desk drawer and pulled out what had become her reference book for the past life work. She flipped to the dedication page of *Many Lives, Many Masters* to again read the message her grandmother had inscribed there.

Little love, Your journey to how past lives collide with current lifetimes has begun. May this book help foster enlightenment and ignite passion for the work that has for decades "fed" me spiritually, emotionally, and physically.

Sophia heard the front door clang open in the waiting room. She put the book back in her desk drawer and went to find Lorraine standing in front of the doorway wearing a much different attire than their last session. While the prior week's clothing had been conservative, Sophia could only describe today's short skirt, tight-fitting blouse and wedge heels as risqué. Rather than wearing her long, auburn hair in a tight bun on her head today, it hung over her shoulders.

At what was likely a surprised expression on Sophia's face, Lorraine looked down at the outfit she wore and burst into tears.

Sophia walked across the waiting room and gently placed her hands on the woman's shoulders. "Whatever is wrong, we can talk it out. Let's go to my office, shall we?"

Once they were in Sophia's office and she had shut the door, she pointed to the couch next to the fountain she ran during sessions.

Lorraine motioned to sit down, but then cried out, "Oh, no! My purse!"

"Did you misplace it?"

Lorraine looked at her wild-eyed. "I don't know. It might be in my car."

"Why don't you go take a look and set your mind at rest."

Lorraine scurried out of the room and down the hall. Sophia waited, glancing at the clock to see that they were fifteen minutes late already. Fortunately, when Lorraine came rushing back, she held a purse in her hands.

"I see you found it," said Sophia. "Please close the door behind you."

Lorraine did as instructed, then sat on the couch and put her purse on the floor. "I'm sorry I was late, Dr. Strand. It's been," she paused, "a day." Tears started to form in her eyes once again.

"That's perfectly alright, but we do have to stop at eleven as scheduled. And I'll have to charge you for the full hour."

The woman nodded as Sophia handed her a box of tissue.

"Now, let's start with today. You're very emotional and seem scattered. Would you like to tell me what happened?"

Lorraine wiped her eyes and gently blew her nose. "Today started out quite nice. Stan, my husband, and I had a nice morning. We even had time to eat breakfast together before he went into the office, which doesn't always happen."

Sophia waited, and when Lorraine didn't continue, she asked, "And then?"

Lorraine threw her hands up in exasperation. "Stan left for work, and I was planning on filling out some job applications when he called."

"He, meaning your husband's colleague with whom you've been having an affair?"

Lorraine stamped a foot on the floor. "Yes."

Sophia waited for her to continue.

"I shouldn't have picked up the phone, but I did. And the next thing you know, I've agreed to...," she trailed off.

"Did you agree to meet with him?" asked Sophia.

"No, much worse. I let him talk me into a rendezvous, that's what he calls them, with a friend of his visiting from out of town." She took a handful of tissue out of the box as tears began streaming down her face in earnest.

"I must ask you this, Lorraine. Is your husband's colleague threatening or coercing you in any way to meet these men?"

She threw up her hands again. "That is the crazy thing about this! He obviously could hold the fact that we've been having an affair over me, and he has said things at times to let me know he could tell Stan, but somehow he talks me into these things. It's almost like I'm in a trance." She met Sophia's eyes. "I know you asked if I have a history of mental illness. By now you're probably thinking I lied, but I swear I'm not lying. Before I met Conrad, I was living a perfectly happy life. There is something about this man that just pulls me toward him, and then I do whatever he wants." Her shoulders began shaking as she buried her face in the tissue.

"I do believe you." Sophia glanced at the clock. "I am going to have you lie back and try to relax while I start a regression meditation. It is my belief that your behavior with this man is rooted in a past life. We can't do a very long regression, but we can take a look at where and when this may have all started. If nothing else, the meditation will help you calm down."

Lorraine looked relieved as she lay back on the couch and closed her eyes. "I'll do anything to feel even a tiny bit calmer. I'm ready, Dr. Strand."

Sophia wasn't sure if Lorraine was in fact ready, but regressing her seemed the only way to begin to untangle what was causing her to unravel. She shut the blinds, then sat down in the armchair across from

Lorraine and put her phone on a side table. "I'm going to tape our session."

Lorraine nodded. "Whatever you want, Dr. Strand."

"Before I get started on the meditation that will lead you to that past life, I want to review quickly the circumstances that have led up to your uncharacteristic behavior in recent months."

"Okay," Lorraine murmured.

"According to what you shared with me during your first session, you met this man at a dinner party that you and your husband held about a year ago at your house."

"That's right," said Lorraine. "His name is Conrad."

"When you both happened to be in the kitchen alone, you felt a strong pull toward Conrad, whom you hadn't met until that night. He apparently felt a pull toward you, as well, and you ended up having sex in the pantry with this man while the guests were in the other room."

Lorraine's face reddened. "Yes."

Since then, you have been drawn to Conrad for reasons you don't understand, and he has set you up with other men, let's say, for companionship reasons. You have followed through but are at a loss as to why. And your husband, Stan, as far as you know, knows nothing about this."

Lorraine sighed and opened her eyes. "When you put it that way, it all sounds crazy enough to get me committed, but yes."

"I'm just reviewing for the sake of the recorded treatment records and to ensure I understand the circumstances," said Sophia. "You have also had no history of being sexually molested or raped, and you have no history of mental illness. Up until this experience, you've been faithful to your husband, with whom you've been married for five years."

"Stan and I have been happy. I mean, we've had our differences, like all married couples, but he's good to me. Which makes this so terrible."

"Right now, I want you to take several deep breaths and try to forget for the moment how badly you feel about your actions and remind yourself that you're here to get to the bottom of this so that you can stop the behavior. Can you do that?"

Lorraine nodded and closed her eyes.

Sophia set her phone to play the sound of light rain and began the meditation.

"Take several deep breaths," said Sophia. "As you do so, let the air flow through your body and out your fingers and toes. Picture the air as gray or black as it leaves your body, taking all tension and anxiety from you. The air that you breathe in is light and refreshing. Now we will begin muscle relaxation, starting at the neck and shoulders. Feel your neck release and your shoulders sink down as you relax into the couch. Breathing, breathing. At the same time, feel your face relax, from your forehead to your chin. Next, we're going to focus on easing tension in your chest."

After a few minutes, Sophia noted that Lorraine had begun to breathe more deeply and her body had relaxed. "Now we're going to take a journey back in time to the first place that your subconscious wishes to show us," said Sophia. "We will walk through a series of doorways. You'll see one doorway in the distance that is purple. That is the door you will pass through where you will see what you came here to see today. You are nearing the doorway. When you arrive, reach out and turn the handle and open the door and step through. Tell me what you see when you enter."

Sophia waited, watching as Lorraine's brow furrowed. A long few moments ticked by before she finally spoke, her voice pleading, "Vincent, please, don't. I've tried. I really have, but the men don't want to pay that much." Her body visibly cringed. "I'm not hiding any of the money. I swear." More moments passed, then Lorraine's head jerked, and her hand flew to her cheek. "Please, I'll do better. I promise. I don't have anywhere else to go. The streets will eat me alive. You said so yourself."

Sophia watched as the woman began to calm down and her shoulders stopped shaking. When several moments passed and she didn't say anything, Sophia asked, "Where are you?"

"I'm in the bathroom trying to get myself together before I have to see another john."

"Did Vincent hurt you?"

"Yes."

"How did he hurt you?"

"He slapped me and then punched me in the stomach really hard." Her hands went to her abdomen. "It still hurts."

"Who is Vincent to you?"

Lorraine startled Sophia by opening her eyes and looking at her. "He's my pimp, of course. Who are you?"

Sophia measured her words carefully. "I'm here to help you. What is your name?"

"Suzette. But sometimes the girls and the johns call me Suzy." Sophia noted that she had what sounded like a Chicago accent.

"What year is it?"

Surprise flashed across Lorraine's eyes again. "Why are you asking me that? You don't know?"

"I'm just checking some facts," said Sophia. "Like I said, I'm here to help you."

Lorraine closed her eyes and rested her head back on the sofa. "It's 1946."

"How old are you?"

"Seventeen, but Vincent thinks I'm eighteen."

"How long have you been with Vincent and the other girls?"

The woman sighed. "It seems like forever, but only six months or so."

Sophia's phone pinged once, signaling their session was almost up.

"Does your stomach feel any better?"

"Yes, it usually feels better after a few minutes."

"I'm going to bring you back to the present now," said Sophia. "I want you to find the purple door and start walking toward it. When you come back through the purple door, you will be heading down a path to the here and now. Listen to the sound of my voice as it guides you. I'm going to count backward from ten. When I reach one, you will be back in 2021. Ten, nine, eight, seven, keep walking, six, five, four, three, two, one. Now slowly open your eyes. You are here in present day Orange."

Sophia turned off the sound of rain as Lorraine came to. It took a moment for her to open her eyes. She seemed confused at first, but then she gasped. "I saw him. But he didn't look like him. I mean it was him, but it wasn't him." She sat up and swung her legs around to sit on the edge of the sofa, her expression animated.

"You are referring to seeing Conrad?"

"Yes." She shook her head as if to clear it, then exclaimed, "I was talking to him!" Further thoughts and then she put her hands on her stomach and frowned. "He hit me in the stomach." Then she put a hand on her cheek. "And he slapped me."

"Do you remember anything else. Who he was to you? His name?"

Lorraine shook her head. "It's hazy."

Sophia's phone buzzed, indicating that the session was over. She picked it up and stopped recording. "You mentioned one name, which was Vincent. We're out of time today. At your next session, we can start with me playing the recording for you."

Disappointment flashed across Lorraine's face, but she stood and Sophia followed suit. "Thank you, Dr. Strand. I sincerely mean that. Even though I'm not entirely clear on what just occurred, one thing is certain at this point. I've known Conrad before." She put her hand to her stomach. "And whatever happened wasn't good. Somehow knowing that I have known him before helps. I can come back tomorrow morning if you have an opening."

Sophia walked over to her desk and flipped open her calendar. "Does ten am work?"

"Yes, it does," said Lorraine.

"Please be on time so we can make the most of your hour."

"I will. Conrad isn't going to make me late again. Knowing he hurt me before, I'm thinking I break ties with him."

"I know you are frustrated with the situation, but I wouldn't advise any grand gestures with Conrad right now, or pronouncements," warned Sophia. "We don't know the extent of what occurred in that past lifetime that is informing this lifetime."

When Lorraine gave her a puzzled look, Sophia explained. "It's important to remember that you aren't the only actor in this play, to use an analogy. Conrad could be volatile. You've said that your husband doesn't know about the affair with him. If you confront Conrad now, he could make good on his threat and respond by telling Stan."

Lorraine looked up at the ceiling. "What do you advise I do, then?"

"Put him off if he contacts you and wants to meet or asks you to meet with anyone else," said Sophia. "Say you aren't feeling well or have other demanding priorities—but be vague."

Lorraine nodded. "I can do that. And it won't be a lie. I'm not feeling well about many things right now."

"Let me walk you out," said Sophia.

When she watched Lorraine head into the parking lot, Sophia gasped as a vintage car drove up beside her. But then Lorraine turned and walked right through the vehicle, and Sophia realized it was an apparition.

Chapter 3

That evening when she, Teddy, and Cerise piled into her car, Sophia glanced in the rearview mirror as she backed out of the carport and saw Teddy take his girlfriend's hand. Was she nervous?

"Teddy may have painted a larger-than-life picture of his great grandmother, but I assure you, she is really a softy. And she's going to love you, Cerise," said Sophia, meeting the girl's eyes in the mirror.

At the smile of relief that covered her face, Sophia was glad she had spoken up.

"My mom's right," said Teddy reassuringly. "My great grandma is kind of scary at first, but honestly, she's really nice."

Sophia laughed. "Teddy has a way with words. My grandmother has never been scary. I think the word he was looking for is imposing."

Cerise giggled. As she did so, Sophia was struck by a vision of the three of them standing looking out onto a field of wildflowers. Sophia was speaking to them about the land—telling them it would be theirs one day. Then, suddenly, someone stepped up behind her and laid a hand on her shoulder. It was Phillip.

"Mom, I thought you were supposed to take the 55 to get to the airport?"

Sophia gasped to see that she had passed the freeway onramp. "Hold on, I'm going to make a U-turn."

"My mom zones out sometimes," said Teddy.

Sophia had stopped at a light, positioned in the left lane so she could make a quick turn. "Teddy!" she cried, meeting his eyes in the rearview mirror.

"No offense, Mom, but sometimes it's like you've gone somewhere else."

"I think about my work sometimes, that's all."

Teddy grinned. "Oh, and she also constantly reads my mind. My great grandmother does, too."

Fifteen minutes later, they pulled onto MacArthur Avenue and were soon driving into John Wayne Airport. "We're looking for British Airways," said Sophia. "Your great grandmother is going to come out to the curb. I'll need you to jump out and get her bags."

"What is your great grandmother's name?" asked Cerise.

"I don't know," said Teddy. "I always call her Grandma. Mom?"

"Ophelia."

Sophia spotted her grandmother standing on the curb and pulled up and stopped. She wore a silver scarf wrapped around her head of dark hair, and a flowing black pantsuit accented with splashes of silver. Even at her age—which Sophia wasn't sure of and had never asked—her grandmother was striking.

When their eyes met, admiration and love washed through Sophia. Teddy hopped out and greeted her, then opened the front passenger door. Her grandmother got in, a warm smile on her face. "Sophia," she greeted her. Then she turned toward the back seat and said, "This must be the lovely Cerise that Teddy can't stop talking about."

Blushing, Cerise extended her hand. "It is so nice to meet you, Ophelia."

Her grandmother took Cerise's hand in hers and gave it a few pats. "It is very nice to meet you, as well."

After situating her things, Teddy slammed the trunk shut, then hopped back in. "And we're off," he said.

Sophia laughed as she headed out of the airport. "Your father used to say that."

"He did? I don't think I've ever said that before. It just popped out."

Sophia and her grandmother laughed in unison.

"What's so funny?" asked Teddy.

"Oh, nothing," said Sophia, glancing back to see for a moment Phillip's face next to his son's.

An hour later, after her grandmother had put her things in Teddy's room, where she'd be staying while he slept in the den, and he had left to take Cerise home, Sophia asked, "Would you like a cup of tea? I have chamomile fresh from Cathy's garden."

Her grandmother had showered and now wore a robe, her hair moist. She pulled out a stool at the kitchen island and sat down. "That would be lovely, thank you."

Sophia put the kettle on to boil, then took teacups from the cupboard and got out the honey pot.

"Cerise is a lovely girl. She and Teddy seem very natural together."

Sophia leaned against the island and sighed. "They do."

Her grandmother pulled a cup toward her. "But you are still worried about her breaking his heart?"

Sophia contemplated. "Not so much that, just..." The kettle started to squeal and she turned it off, then added two scoops of tea. "Honestly, Grandmother, I have no idea why I'm worried. She is a sweetheart and has shown no signs that she would be careless with Teddy's heart." She placed the teakettle on a trivet, and the fresh scent of steeping chamomile filled the air.

"That smells wonderful," said her grandmother. She pointed to the stool on the other side of the island. "Sit."

Sophia did as she was told, slumping into the chair.

"Has Phillip been visiting you?"

"Yes, more often than usual."

"And you're concerned that he is trying to warn you about Teddy and Cerise?"

"I think maybe that is it. Watching them, I can't help but think about Phillip and myself in those early days, and then..."

"He died. So, your thought process is, will something terrible now happen to Teddy or Cerise to break up this wonderful union?"

Sophia poured tea into her grandmother's cup, then her own. "I think that's it. I know rationally that their story isn't Phillip's and my story, but how do I stop myself?"

Her grandmother took a sip of tea. "This is delicious. I think you can stop yourself by facing the lingering lessons that you still haven't addressed regarding your time with Phillip in this lifetime, and past lifetimes. Have you been doing more regressions to past lifetimes with him?"

"I was for a while but haven't recently. I've been busy at work, including starting with a new past life client."

"How is that going?"

"I've only had a couple of sessions with her, but it's a very interesting case. A bit overwhelming to be honest."

"How so?"

Sophia was always careful not to break patient confidentiality when she asked questions of her grandmother, who had done this work for decades. "Since meeting someone with whom she seems to have had a traumatic past life, she has been acting impulsively and compulsively—extremely out of character. Most disturbingly, her actions are putting her in dangerous situations. Have you seen that before?"

"Yes, often. I'm sure you've ruled out deeper mental health issues."

"Yes, although if the past life regression doesn't help her, I will refer her to a psychiatrist."

Her grandmother took a sip of tea. "I think the past life regression will help her." She yawned. "Forgive me, little love, I've done my best to stay up, but I need some sleep."

Sophia glanced at the clock on the wall. "It's nine o'clock. I'd say that's a perfect time to turn in."

Her grandmother got up and gave Sophia a kiss on the cheek. "I'll see you in the morning, then?"

"Yes. I have a session in the morning with the new client I just mentioned, but not until ten. Teddy has the day off school, so perhaps you and he can do something during that time. By noon, I'm all yours. We've planned some fun outings."

Her grandmother's smile widened. "I look forward to it."

After her grandmother went into Teddy's room and closed the door, Sophia remembered what Phillip had said to her that morning about her grandmother's visit being significant. She had meant to ask her what she thought of that. It would have to wait until morning.

Chapter 4

Sophia awoke and glanced at the clock. Eight am. Then she remembered that her grandmother was there. Eager to talk to her, she hopped out of bed and made her way to the kitchen, but she was nowhere in sight. Had she gone out for a walk? There was motion in the hallway and Teddy walked in.

"Morning, Mom. Any coffee made?"

"I just got up. Where's your grandmother?"

"She's probably sleeping in from jet lag." Teddy fished the coffee filters out of the cupboard and placed one in the coffee maker. He glanced at Sophia. "You want any?"

Sophia nodded absently. "Sure."

"Where are we going this afternoon?"

Sophia leaned against the counter, thinking how when her grandmother came to visit, she was always up long before anyone else. Should she tap on her door to see if she needed anything?"

"Mom?"

"Yes, oh, where are we going? What's first on the list we made?"

"Good morning," said a voice behind them. "What is first on the list?"

Sophia swung around to see her grandmother fully dressed for the day in black slacks and a bright red sweater. Many older women couldn't pull off such a bold outfit, but her grandmother wore it with style. At the sight of her up and looking well rested, relief swept through Sophia. What was wrong with her? So jumpy and anxious about seemingly nothing.

Teddy answered since Sophia didn't speak up. "The first thing on the list is going to Sherman Gardens in Corona Del Mar."

"Well, by all means, let's start with number one on the list. That sounds delightful." Her grandmother raised an eyebrow at Sophia as she sat down at the kitchen island. "You're quiet, did you not sleep well last night?"

"I slept well, but a little while ago, I had a strange sense of...," Sophia stopped herself, noting that Teddy listened intently as he handed her a cup of coffee. "Teddy, could you put the kettle on for your grandmother's tea?"

As Teddy went to heat the water, her grandmother turned her attention to Sophia. "Come sit. What is it, little love?"

Sophia shrugged her shoulders as she sat on a stool facing her grandmother. "I'm not sure." She glanced at Teddy, busy filling the tea kettle, and said in a low tone, "He came to me yesterday and said something."

Her grandmother nodded for her to go on.

"He said that your visit would be significant for us—you, me, and Teddy."

"Very interesting."

Teddy's phone rang, and he answered it.

Sophia raised her eyebrows at her grandmother. "That's all you have to say about that?"

Teddy's voice became intimate as he walked down the hallway and went into the den.

Her grandmother smiled. "He must be talking to Cerise."

Sophia took a sip of her coffee and nodded.

"It's not always time to know everything," her grandmother said simply.

"Meaning, you have no idea what Phillip meant by his comment?"

The teakettle began squealing, and her grandmother got up. "I'll get it." She took out a box of Earl Grey, then tore open a teabag and filled the cup with hot water and brought it back with her.

Sophia waited, still feeling unusually pensive.

Once her grandmother was settled, she said, "You are assuming that Phillip's message is a bad thing, but what if it is a good thing?"

Sophia sat back and relaxed a bit. "I hadn't thought of that."

"Often, people get messages from the other side and assume they are doomsday prophecies," said her grandmother, who picked up the teabag and dipped it back into the water, releasing the scent of bergamot. "It could very well be a wonderful turning point of some sort."

"But you don't know what that turning point is?"

Her grandmother smiled. "No, I don't. We aren't supposed to know everything all at once—our human selves, that is. We are meant to receive the information and the experiences as they are doled out to us. That's what living this human experience is all about. If we were told the end of the story right now, what would be the point of living through to the end?"

Sophia considered. "That makes sense. But sometimes..." She didn't finish the thought.

Her grandmother reached over and took Sophia's hand in hers. "Sometimes, you want to skip to the end of the book just to make sure that tragedy doesn't befall the hero or heroine."

Sophia swallowed and nodded. "I think that's an accurate assessment of what I'm feeling."

Her grandmother tightened her grip on Sophia's hand. "Phillip's loss will always haunt you, but it needn't define you. And it hasn't. You've built a wonderful life for yourself and Teddy. However, it seems that there is one thing holding you back, and that is the fear of something equally as devastating befalling you or someone you love at any minute. Is that accurate, do you think?"

Sophia nodded, feeling tears pricking at the back of her eyes.

"The best thing I've found to deal with such anxiety is to ask myself what I would tell a client."

Sophia gazed at her grandmother's hands enveloping her own, then back into her wise eyes. "That's a good idea. I'd tell my client to enjoy the moment, the day, for what it is, and not worry about things that probably won't happen, anyway."

Her grandmother smiled and let go of Sophia's hand to take a sip of tea. "Excellent advice. I'd suggest taking it. And let's just wait and see what wonderful significance comes from my trip for all of us."

Sophia nodded. "I can do that."

"Good. I'm hungry. Do you have any oatmeal, or eggs?"

Teddy walked back into the room then. "I was going to make you Huevos Rancheros, if that sounds good Grandma."

"It sounds delicious. After breakfast, what would you like to do this morning while your mother is attending to her client?"

"How about we walk around the Plaza? I know you like to visit the antique shops," suggested Teddy.

"Splendid idea," she replied.

Sophia picked up her coffee cup and stood. "Now that you both have a plan of action, I better get ready for the office." As she walked down the hallway toward her bedroom, she smiled when she heard her grandmother say, "Will these eggs be spicy? I do like things on the spicy side. Did I tell you about the time I went to Portugal and cooked with a famous chef known for using extra hot chili peppers in his dishes?"

Sophia arrived at the office to find Cathy in the waiting room with a measuring tape in one hand.

"I thought you were out for today. Didn't your grandmother come in last night?"

"She did," said Sophia, eyeing the measuring tape. "A new client is in a bit of a crisis, so I'm doing one session, then leaving for the rest of the day."

Cathy pointed to the far wall. "I'm thinking of installing a wall fountain. The water is so peaceful, and I really like yours. What do you think?"

"I think it's a great idea."

"How's your grandmother doing?" asked Cathy. "I'd love to see her when she's here."

"Teddy and I want to have you and Chuck over for dinner, as well as Professor Kirten. I think you've met him."

"Oh, yes, the retired philosophy professor who knew Phillip. He's a delightful man." She grinned at Sophia. "Are you doing some matchmaking?"

Sophia laughed. "I think my grandmother and the professor will really enjoy meeting each other, and who knows, they might just hit it off. Either way, he makes a great dinner guest. So, what do you say? How about Sunday night?"

"I'll check with Chuck, but I think we are free."

The door opened just then, and Lorraine stood on the threshold, her hair disheveled and her expression wild-eyed. "Hi, Dr. Strand, I think I might be early."

Sophia glanced at the clock on the wall, which read a quarter to ten. "You are, but that's better than being late. Have a seat while I get my office opened, and then I'll be back to get you."

Five minutes later, Sophia went back to the waiting room to usher Lorraine to her office. As they passed through the hallway, Sophia felt tension rolling off Lorraine and thought that it was probably a good thing they had a little extra time today.

"Have a seat," said Sophia, gesturing to the couch. She had already turned on the fountain, and its soothing, trickling sound echoed in the room.

Lorraine sat, and as if just realizing her appearance was haphazard, ran her hands along the sides of her head to tame her mane. Then she clasped her hands together on her lap and met Sophia's gaze. "Thank you for seeing me today. I..." she looked down at her hands, then sighed, and raised her head once again. "I didn't take your advice regarding staying away from Conrad."

"That's not surprising."

"It's not?"

Sophia shook her head. "No, it isn't." She thought for a moment as to how to frame things so that Lorraine would understand. "I know this whole past life thing is new to you. There are many layers to this—many nuances. At first glance, it appears to be straightforward. You knew this person in a prior lifetime, sometimes many years ago, but I've found that it is far from straightforward."

Sophia paused as Lorraine digested her words and appeared to calm down a bit. She unclasped her hands, and said, "I'm beginning to see how complicated it is. When I learned at our last session that I'd known Conrad before and that he had hurt me, I thought it was a no-brainer to just cut things off and be done with him. But that didn't work out so well."

Chapter 5

"May I ask what happened during your meeting with Conrad?" asked Sophia.

Lorraine's bottom lip trembled. "I told him we needed to meet, and we did at this motel where we get together. I was mad as hell and ready to break things off. I got there first and really believed I was going to end things, but when he came in..." She stopped and took a deep breath and continued. "When he came in and said that I looked like hell, I don't know what happened. My resolve just crumbled. I became self-conscious. It was as if I had to please him or something." She threw up her hands. "This is so crazy on so many levels. What kind of an idiot am I?"

Silence filled the room for a few moments.

"Did you have sex with him?" asked Sophia.

Lorraine nodded. "Can you believe it? The man tells me I look like hell, and the next thing I know, I'm in bed with him. Even though I didn't have a chance to say anything about breaking it off, it was as if he knew."

"He sensed that you were pulling away."

"Exactly! So, he insults me, and I feel like I have to prove myself."

"Did he ask anything else of you?"

Lorraine frowned. "Yes, another of his clients is coming in tonight, and stupid me, I told him I'd meet with him. I'm hopeless, Dr. Strand!"

"First of all, you're not hopeless. I assure you that we can get to the bottom of this push and pull between you and Conrad. But it's going to take time, and you must stay away from him as much as possible for this to work. As I mentioned, this type of treatment is not straightforward, nor is the healing process that accompanies it. You have known each other over many lifetimes. Things aren't going to get fixed in one or two sessions."

Lorraine gave Sophia a small smile. "My mother says that one of my biggest problems is not being patient enough with myself."

"Your mother is a wise woman." Sophia picked up her phone. "I want you to listen to your last session before I regress you."

Lorraine eyed Sophia's phone with some trepidation as she started playing the recording. As soon as she heard her voice with the Chicago accent, she gasped. "I sound so different!"

After the recording finished, Lorraine put her hands on her stomach. "When I was listening to how I got punched by Conrad, I could feel the pain in my stomach. Is that weird?"

"Not at all," said Sophia. "Hearing yourself back then likely stirred up memories from that lifetime. And that's a good thing. Because the more we understand from that past lifetime and you process it, the more you will be able to clear things up in this lifetime. Past life regression therapy is similar to therapy focused on unearthing trauma in this lifetime. You must unpack the trauma and examine it before you can process what happened and then discard the parts that no longer work for you. If that makes sense."

Lorraine appeared relieved. "That does make sense. It's good to know there is a process to this, even if it's not a transparent one."

Sophia smiled. "Are you ready to regress and see what else occurred during that lifetime?"

Lorraine lay back on the couch. "I'm ready."

Sophia set her phone to play the sound of light rain and started. Before long, Lorraine's breathing slowed. When she was in a relaxed state, Sophia began the journey back in time.

"You will see in the distance a familiar sight. The purple door. When you reach it, you are going to walk through it and step into another time and place of significance to you in this lifetime. Take your time approaching the door, knowing you are prepared for what you will see on the other side. The experience will enlighten your now. Slowly, slowly, you've arrived at the door. Take a deep breath as you prepare to open the door."

Lorraine inhaled deeply and exhaled.

"Very good," said Sophia. "Now I want you to reach out and open the door. When you do, step through the doorway and let me know what you see on the other side."

"He's going to be mad. I just know it," said Lorraine suddenly.

"I'm here to guide you," Sophia assured her. "He might be mad, but he can't hurt you. That was then and this is now. You're on a journey to the truth."

"I've turned the knob. I'm going in."

Sophia waited a few beats, then asked, "Are you in?"

"I am," said Lorraine, the Chicago accent back now. "This is a hell of a mess."

"What is?" asked Sophia.

"Why, the clothing strung all about, don't you know? The girls must have left in a hurry. No one is here." Lorraine yelped then and raised her arms above her head.

Suzette knew as soon as she saw the disarray in the room that something was wrong. Even in a hurry to get to a job, the girls never left things this messy. Vincent demanded everything in order. And where was Rand? Vincent never left the place empty. She was picking some clothing off the floor when the door crashed open and a police officer stormed through, followed by two others. They had their guns drawn, so she raised her arms.

Once they determined no one else was there, one of the officers harnessed his weapon and said, "You can put your arms down." He was a tall man with light-colored hair and kind eyes. "Do you live here?"

"Yes," said Suzette, who wrapped her arms around herself as she stood there. One of the other officers pulled open drawers in the room, and she could hear the other in Vincent's room.

"We're looking for a Vincent McMurray. Is he here?"

Suzette became mute at the mention of Vincent's name. He had said that if anyone ever asked for him—in particular, the police—she was to claim not to know him.

"How old are you?" asked the officer when she didn't answer.

"I'm nineteen."

He scrutinized her for a moment, then repeated, "How old are you, really?"

Suzette answered, her voice choked, "Seventeen, but I'll be eighteen next month."

Another officer returned to the room then, and said, "No one else on the premises. It looks like they left in a hurry. And nothing in McMurray's room." He gestured to Suzette. "Anything?"

"Not much. She's underage, so we need to take her in."

The officer with the kind eyes asked Suzette, "Do you have a jacket? Night is coming on quick, and it's cold out there."

She nodded and went to the closet to pull out a coat, slipping it over the short dress she wore.

"Am I under arrest?" she asked as he led her to a police car parked in front of the brownstone.

"Not at the moment. We'll talk more at the station."

When they got to the station a few minutes later, the officer sat her down in a chair facing a metal desk stacked with papers and left for a moment, returning with a cup of coffee that he handed to her. The cup felt good on Suzette's hands; warm and encouraging.

"You hungry?" he asked. "I can order a pizza."

The thought of pizza set Suzette's stomach to rumbling, but then she remembered what Vincent had warned. The johns didn't want fat girls.

When she didn't reply, he picked up the phone and dialed, smiling when a voice came on the line. "Georgia, you're working tonight, good. Can I get my usual?" He laughed at her response, then said, "I'm at my desk, so have Antonio bring it up, and put it on my tab."

Once he'd hung up, the man turned his attention to Suzette and said, "The pizza place is in the shop next door, so it won't be too long. We haven't been formally introduced. My name is Officer Pete. What's your name?"

Suzette decided she should be honest. "My real name is Evelyn but people call me Suzette or Suzy here."

The officer had taken out a pad and pencil. "Evelyn what? And where are you from?"

She thought about Vincent's insistence on forgetting where she came from and never telling anyone, but did that apply right now?"

"I'm going to find out one way or another," said Officer Pete quietly. "The easiest way is for you to just tell me."

Suzette nodded. "My last name is Harquest, and I'm from Peoria.

"As in Peoria, Illinois?"

"Yes, sir."

"How did you happen to make your way to Chicago? Peoria is three hours from here."

Suzette shifted in her chair, then once again decided honesty was best. "I ran away from home on the bus."

He nodded as he made notes on a pad. "How long ago was that?"

"Six months ago, I think."

He looked up from writing and raised his eyebrows. "You think?"

"It was fall when I came. Before the first snowfall."

Officer Pete appeared thoughtful. "That would have been mid-September. It's April 4 right now, so you've been here seven months. Does that sound right?"

"That sounds right."

"Tell me why you ran away from home. And did you run away from a family—mother and father?"

Suzette took a sip of coffee, then said, "My father died when I was a baby. Until a year ago, it was just me and my mom."

He stopped; the pencil poised over the paper. "What happened a year ago?"

"My mom got a boyfriend."

Officer Pete nodded slowly. "And things didn't go well with you and the boyfriend?"

"No sir," said Suzette, the anger she'd felt the night she left home boiling up inside of her now.

"Did he hurt you?"

"He never hit me, if that's what you're asking, but he was constantly yelling at me." She glanced over his shoulder to see a boy approaching carrying a pizza box.

"Thank you, Antonio, just set it on the desk," said Officer Pete as he pulled a dollar bill out of his pants pocket and pressed it into the boy's hand.

When Officer Pete lifted the lid of the box, the scent of pepperoni and onion made Suzette realize just how hungry she was. He pulled some napkins out of his desk drawer and handed her one. "I'm going to have a piece or two, and then we can resume. Help yourself."

Suzette smiled the first genuine smile she could remember having since she arrived in town and reached for a piece of pizza. "Thank you."

When Suzette bit into the slice, she held back a groan. This had to be the absolute best pizza she had ever had. She tried not to eat too quickly, but the hunger she'd been repressing for months took over, and she ended up devouring four slices. When she finished and wiped her mouth, feeling embarrassed by having been such a glutton, she was about to apologize when Officer Pete smiled and said, "I'm glad you got some food in you. You're looking on the thin side. Now, let's talk about what happened when you arrived in Chicago."

Suzette was about to continue with her story, even telling the officer the truth, when an older man she'd seen Vincent with on multiple occasions came storming toward them. "The interview with my client is over," said the man, his fat middle straining against a gray suit.

Officer Pete stood then and faced the man. "She has informed me that she is a minor and a runaway. So, you're going to have to wait until I sort this out."

The man set a briefcase on an empty chair and flipped it open, pulling out a form. "The minor has been remanded into my custody by her parents." He handed the papers to the surprised officer. "That's from Judge Nielson. If you have any problems with the paperwork, take it up with him. I'm getting the young lady out of here. It's way past her bedtime."

Officer Pete snorted. "Real fatherly of you. I know what kind of game you and McMurray are playing, and I'm going to get to the bottom of it."

The lawyer motioned for Suzette to stand, then turned to Officer Pete. "No game, officer. Just doing my job." He took Suzette by the arm.

"I'm going to check into this," said Officer Pete. "If these papers aren't on the up-and-up, I'm coming for you and your boss. Where is McMurray, anyway?"

Suzette felt the man stiffen. "If you are referring to my client, Vincent McMurray, I'm not at liberty to discuss his whereabouts. He is currently vacationing, which as far as I know isn't a crime."

"It is a crime if he's vacationing with underaged girls," said Officer Pete.

"I am not aware of any other underaged girls. If you don't mind, we're leaving."

"Oh, I do mind, but we'll be talking again."

The lawyer swung Suzette around and marched her toward the doorway, his hand so tight on her arm, she thought he might break it.

Chapter 6

When Lorraine put a hand on her arm and winced, Sophia decided to bring her back. "It's time to return to the here and now," she said softly. "I want you to locate the purple door and begin walking toward it. I will begin counting backwards from twenty as you head toward the door. Slowly, slowly, you are nearing the door. Twenty, nineteen, eighteen, you are getting closer, seventeen, sixteen, fifteen, soon you will be at the door, fourteen, thirteen, twelve, eleven, ten, nine, you are just about there, eight, seven, six, five, get ready to walk back into the now, four, three, two, one. Your hand is on the doorknob. Turn it and return to Orange, California, 2021."

Sophia waited as Lorraine's eyes fluttered open and she lay there for a moment, looking up at the ceiling. After several long moments, she said, "I was talking to him."

"Who, Conrad?"

Lorraine sat up on the loveseat and faced her, a mixture of shock and surprise on her face. "No, my husband, Stan."

Interesting, thought Sophia. "Who was Stan to you in the prior lifetime?"

"A police officer named Pete. He arrested me. How odd that in this lifetime Stan is a lawyer."

"That is interesting, but not uncommon or coincidental," said Sophia.

Lorraine brushed her hair away from her face. "Why do you say that?"

"I've found that people often gravitate toward similar occupations from lifetime to lifetime. It's not to say that you would always be a police officer but you may come back and work in the same field. What type of law does Stan do?"

Lorraine cleared her throat and replied, "Family law." She put her head in her hands. "This is all so confusing, Dr. Strand. Do you think I'll ever get a handle on this?"

"I believe that you will," said Sophia. "We just need to continue to delve into what happened in that prior lifetime. Besides getting arrested by Stan, who it looks like you were calling Officer Pete, what else happened during your regression?"

Lorraine closed her eyes. "I was taken to the police station. I had been out on a job, and the john dropped me off at the brownstone where me and the other girls all lived with Conrad, whose name was Vincent then. When I got there, it looked like he and the girls had left in a rush. That's when the police came looking for him and found me."

Sophia's phone pinged, indicating the session was coming to a close. "Although I know you don't feel as if you've resolved much yet, I have to remind you this is only your second session, and we have learned quite a bit today," said Sophia. "For one, that Stan was in that lifetime with you. That is very significant." Sophia appraised Lorraine, whose shoulders were no longer tight. "You look a lot less frazzled than when you came in earlier."

Lorraine picked up her purse. "Now that you mentioned it, I do feel less tense. I think I will go home and cook Stan and me a nice dinner for tonight."

Sophia smiled. "That sounds like a lovely idea for today. How about we set up your next session? I am out of the office for the rest of the day and weekend, but I can do Monday at the same time."

"That will be good."

"Great," said Sophia. "Let me walk you out."

They headed down the hallway and stopped in the waiting room, where Lorraine turned to face Sophia. "Thank you, Dr. Strand. I'm so grateful for your help with this. I feel a lot calmer and hopeful. It's Stan and my fifth wedding anniversary tomorrow. I think I'll plan something nice."

Sophia smiled. "That sounds like a wonderful idea. Contact me if you need me."

Lorraine put her purse on her shoulder. "I'm hoping not to have to, but it's good to know you're there."

Sophia watched Lorraine walking toward her car, a spring in her step for the first time since she'd met her.

Back in her office a few moments later, Sophia sat down at her desk to take notes on their session. As she did so, she referred to the tape recording several times. With what Lorraine had said during the regression and then afterward, she was able to piece together what had happened in the prior lifetime.

When she listened to the part where Lorraine had met Officer Pete, her breath caught in her throat. She stopped the recording and returned it to a few seconds before and listened again. She hadn't been imagining it. There was a second voice on the tape. But there had been no one else in the room with them. She backed it up again and pressed play, this time listening intently to what had been said. She heard a man's voice, eerily clear, say, "I will always find you, Suzette. You will never escape me."

A cold breeze crept across Sophia's desk as she realized it had to be Conrad, AKA Vincent.

Chapter 7

It wasn't until later that night that Sophia had a chance to talk to her grandmother privately. Once they'd settled in the living room with cups of chamomile tea, her grandmother said, "While I could talk about what a lovely day today was at Sherman Gardens, let's get straight to the chase, as they say. You want to ask me something. What is it?"

Sophia chuckled. "I can't have any mysteries with you. There is something I've been dying to ask you all day. It came up after my session this morning."

Her grandmother took a sip of tea, then settled it on her lap. "I'm listening."

"Like you taught me, I always record the sessions with the client's knowledge. I'll ask them questions during the regressions as to what is occurring, and those replies and any narration they provide is recorded. But today—this is going to sound crazy—when I was playing back the recording and making notes on the session, I discovered another voice on the tape. I didn't hear it during the session. But there was clearly another person recorded. He even addressed my client in that past lifetime by name."

"Ahh," said her grandmother, "so it has occurred for you as well. It is highly unusual, but it happens."

"What happens?"

"One of the players in the past life, especially those with big personalities and strong feelings, can break through the regression and express desires or sentiments. What did the person say?"

"That he would always find my client, and that she can't escape him."

"Oh, my. That does speak volumes, doesn't it?"

"You mean to say it was literal?"

"Most definitely."

"Would that be for this lifetime or the prior lifetime?"

Her grandmother set her tea on the coffee table. "Most likely, both."

The chill Sophia had felt in her office returned. "Grandmother, I'm not sure I'm up for this situation. This character in her life, he doesn't appear to be a nice man."

"The villains in the story generally aren't. But this isn't the first time you've dealt with a past life regression where one of the players was difficult."

Sophia pondered for a moment. "That's true. I'm not sure what it is about this case that seems so different."

"Every case will be different, and some will be more difficult than others," said her grandmother. "The bottom line is that this person came to you to help her solve these past life struggles for a reason. You have everything you need to help her. You wouldn't have been presented with the challenge if you couldn't overcome it."

Sophia sighed. "I suppose. I just feel so responsible for her well-being."

"As you should. But remember you have assistance from the other side as well."

"You're speaking of Phillip?"

"Phillip is always guiding you, of course, as are the passed on loved ones of those you are helping, and their life guides and angels."

Sophia finished her cup of tea. "That's a good thing for me to keep in mind. It makes me feel much less alone in all of this."

Her grandmother put her arm around Sophia and pulled her close. "I say it quite often, but it bears repeating. You truly are never alone. I know Phillip's early departure left a hole in your life, and that hole can sometimes feel like a chasm, but he is there for you. And one day, there will be someone else. When it's time for both of you to reunite."

Sophia felt great comfort in her grandmother's embrace as she replied, "It's been many years now since his passing, but I still feel so loyal to Phillip."

"One of our greatest strengths is being able to sense, see, and hear those who aren't present on earth, but at the same time that can be a burden. Still, there is much we can learn from those who have passed." Her grandmother patted her shoulder. "It's been a long day. Time for me to go to bed." She picked up her and Sophia's cups and took them to the kitchen.

Sophia decided to unwind in the bathtub before bed. She filled the tub and sprinkled in rose-lavender bath salts, then slid in and leaned back. Resting in the warm, aromatic water, she closed her eyes and thought about what her grandmother had said—that not everything that seemed like an omen was bad news. She knew that her tendency to jump to worst-case scenarios stemmed from losing her mother as a teenager, and then Phillip. She could see now all these years later that those losses made her a better therapist. She helped clients navigate emotions, which tended to be far more difficult to traverse than many realized. Of all the emotions, she had found that clients tended to have the most difficult time overcoming melancholy and regret. Emotions such as sadness and anger were difficult, but they were more extreme and people tended to face them in one way or another. Melancholy and regret tended to eat at you, little by little, she had found. But when clients overcame those feelings, replacing them with gratitude, she found they did so much better.

Sophia closed her eyes and made a conscious effort to remove her therapist hat and relax.

"Angora, my darling, I love the hair, but I'd hurry. We go on in five," said a woman sitting at a dressing table brushing her hair.

"Go on?"

The woman laughed, a high-pitched tinkling sound. Then she flipped her head over and twisted her hair into a knot and began securing it on her head with pins. "You're such a kidder. Please don't tell me you're still pining after that lad who was in the other night. The young ones don't have money. Although, I will admit he was quite a looker with those baby blue eyes."

Sophia didn't say a word, instead jumped when another woman came waltzing in. She wore a black bustier, clip-on stockings, and high heels. On her head sat a bright-red feather headdress.

"Let's go ladies. The crowd is getting restless. You look good Mariah." Then she checked out Sophia. "Hurry up, Angora, and put on your heels. I want you both on time tonight—not two beats behind." She turned and left the room, the sound of trombones tuning up drifting in as the door opened and closed.

Sophia turned to look at herself in her dressing table mirror and gasped to see her face looking back at her, but her hair was blonde and had been braided and twisted on top of her head. She wore bright red lipstick, and her eyes were heavily penciled with black liner. On the vanity in front of her lay a white feather headdress that was smaller than the other woman's. She picked it up and secured it to her head with pins as the music heightened beyond the door—cymbals clashing now.

After sliding her feet into the high heels next to her dressing table, she stood as Mariah outstretched her hand to take Sophia's. Then her partner pushed the door open, and they clacked along a dark hallway toward the sound of the orchestra. A final sharp turn, and they were backstage. The woman with the red headdress stood in front of the still drawn curtain, several other pairs of dancers behind her. Sophia and Mariah took their places, arms outstretched and one long leg in front of the other, as a man's voice from the wings counted down from ten. Then the curtains opened and lights blinded Sophia momentarily as whistles filled the air. The orchestra began playing, and Sophia followed Mariah's lead as they kicked their legs and danced while the audience roared.

It was when they finished and took several bows together, arms interlocked, that Sophia met the eyes of a young, handsome man in the audience wearing a sailor suit. It was Phillip.

Chapter 8

The next morning, Sophia found her grandmother working a crossword puzzle at the kitchen island. She took off her reading glasses and smiled. "Good morning, how did you sleep?"

Sophia yawned as she filled a mug with coffee. "I slept well but for some reason I'm tired, as if I was busy all night."

Her grandmother laughed. "You likely were."

Sophia grabbed the sugar pot and pulled out a stool and sat down. "Busy, how so?"

"We haven't talked about this much, but our souls do take flight at night."

This was the first Sophia had heard about this. "They do? You mean like astral projection?"

Her grandmother set down the pencil and nodded. "Much like astral projection. We go to visit one another in the Light."

Sophia's heart sped up slightly. "So, are you saying that I go to meet Phillip in the Light?"

Her grandmother smiled. "Yes, most certainly. That's why we sometimes wake up feeling tired, as if we've done a workout while sleeping, and why we'll think of someone upon waking."

Sophia added sugar to her cup of coffee. "That is fascinating and in a strange way explains so much." She stirred the sugar in, recalling her experience in the bathtub. "Last night I dozed off in the bath for a while, and I think I inadvertently did a past life regression."

"Do tell. What happened?"

Sophia told her about being a dancer and how Phillip was in the audience.

"That sounds like a fun life."

Teddy walked in and mumbled, "Morning." Then he opened the cupboard and took out a mug.

"How did you sleep?" Sophia asked.

Teddy was about to reply when her grandmother's cellphone rang. "Excuse me, I need to get this." She crossed the room and went out onto the balcony.

Sophia waited as her son set the mug down on the countertop, then gave her a pointed look. "I didn't sleep too well. I had a really weird dream."

"That happens."

"I mean really weird."

Something about the tone of Teddy's voice gave Sophia pause. "How about you sit down and tell me about your dream."

Teddy glanced at the balcony.

"She's probably on with a client and could be awhile."

He poured himself some coffee, then sat down next to her and appeared to be searching for the right words for a moment. "You, me, and a man, who I think was my father, were standing next to a volcano."

Sophia waited.

"It was about to erupt, and dad said that we needed to just stay there and get swallowed up by the volcano. I was scared. Who wouldn't be? But he didn't look scared at all." Teddy's brow furrowed as he reached for the cream. "I mean, is this normal having such a strange, vivid dream? Do I have a death wish or something?"

Sophia suppressed a smile. "Dreams are tricky because they tend to be symbolic. This isn't saying to me that you have a death wish or something bad is going to happen." She waited to see if Teddy would attempt to decipher the dream.

He poured some creamer in his coffee, then his face lit up. "Oh, so not a death wish, but my dad did die."

"Exactly," said Sophia. "And do you see any more similarities between the dream and real life?"

His brow twisted for a moment, then he exclaimed, "He died in an explosion."

"Right, and a volcano would be a type of explosion."

Teddy took a sip of coffee, his face appearing more relaxed. "So, this is more about what happened than what's going to happen?"

Sophia nodded. "It seems so. Although, you mentioned being frightened. That would be a valid feeling, given the circumstances. But are there things in your life right now that frighten you? Besides cleaning your room."

Teddy laughed, then his expression became serious. He looked out at his grandmother and back at Sophia. "If I'm going to be honest, the thing that scares me the most is losing someone I love. Not that I don't love my dad, because I do. I just don't remember him. But If I were to lose you, or grandma, or..."

Sophia finished the sentence for him. "Cerise."

Teddy took a gulp of coffee and nodded. "Yes, Cerise. I can't explain it, Mom. We've only been dating for three months, but it's like I've always known her. If something happened to her, like what happened to you and dad, I don't think I could handle it."

Sophia took a deep breath. "Well, first of all, you would survive, but I don't think Cerise is going anywhere. She's obviously as smitten with you as you are with her."

"You really think so?"

Sophia smiled. "I know so."

"Is this what you and Grandma do all day? Talk to people about their weird dreams and feelings, so they can figure things out?"

"Something like that, yes."

Her grandmother pulled open the balcony door. "What gorgeous weather we have for November. I'd say it's close to eighty degrees out there."

"I vote for heading to the beach and eating lunch there," said Teddy.

"That sounds like a splendid idea," said her grandmother as Sophia's phone rang. She glanced at the screen. It was Lorraine.

"Answer it," said her grandmother. "I think it's important."

Sophia felt the same urgency. She headed for the balcony and answered. As she walked out onto the sunny deck, Lorraine's breathless voice filled the line. "I'm so glad you answered, Dr. Strand. I don't know what to do. Conrad is threatening to tell my husband everything if I don't meet with him. I tried to push him off like you suggested, but he's really angry."

"First of all, take a few deep breaths to calm yourself, Lorraine. You can't make a rational decision or even have a rational thought if you're barely breathing." She waited while Lorraine seemed to be catching her breath, then asked, "Where are you?"

Lorraine's voice sounded slightly less strained. "At home."

"Where is your husband?"

"He's at work, but I think he has a meeting with Conrad today. As I mentioned, they work together."

"In what capacity, exactly? Do you know?" asked Sophia.

"Conrad works for a partner company, so they go to meetings about deals together. That's all I know."

"Even though Conrad scares you, he seems like he is also into self-preservation, and he's not likely to ruin a business meeting over this. I think he's just threatening you to scare you into doing his bidding."

"Are you sure?"

Sophia felt once again that she was in way over her head on this one. She glanced at her grandmother and Teddy talking animatedly in the kitchen. "I know you don't want to hear this, but you might need to tell your husband the truth," she said. "If you do so, then Conrad will no longer hold any power over you."

Lorraine began sobbing on the other end of the phone. "I can't, Dr. Strand. Stan would leave me, and that's just not possible right now. Oh, my god, I can't believe this happened."

Sophia felt one of her knowing feelings then and asked, "Lorraine are you pregnant?"

Silence on the other end of the line, and then Lorraine exclaimed, "How did you know?"

"I've been a therapist for a long time. When did you discover you are pregnant?"

"Yesterday afternoon after I saw you. I took a pregnancy test when I got home, and it was positive. I was able to get in to see my gynecologist, and she confirmed it. I was trying not to bother you, but I feel like I'm losing it, Dr. Strand."

Sophia glanced at her grandmother and Teddy, now in the kitchen preparing breakfast together. "I know I told you that I can't meet until Monday, but I think it would be best for you if I make some time today. Are you free this morning?"

"Yes, I can come whenever you want. Thank you so much, Dr. Strand. I'll pay you double."

When Sophia went back into the house, she could tell by the expressions on their faces that her grandmother and Teddy knew what she was going to say next. "I'm sorry, but I have a client in great distress. Maybe I can catch up with you both at the beach?"

"Of course," said her grandmother. She put her arm around Teddy and pulled him close. "I'll never complain about having my great grandson all to myself."

"We'll be fine," agreed Teddy. "You want some eggs before you go?"

Sophia's stomach was upset from the telephone call. "No, thanks, I'll just grab a banana on my way out."

When Sophia unlocked the office door an hour later, she heard Lorraine's car pull up. She pushed open the door and stepped into the waiting room and flipped on the overhead lights as the woman came rushing in. She had her usually coiffed hair tied back in a loose ponytail and wore jeans and a T-shirt.

"Thanks again," said Lorraine. "I hope I didn't pull you away from anything important."

"You're welcome," said Sophia. "Let's go into my office." She locked the door behind them, then explained, "We're usually not open on Saturdays."

In her office, Sophia turned on the lights and the fountain. "Go ahead and take a seat on the couch."

Lorraine sat and grasped her stomach. "You're a mom, aren't you? That's a photo of you and your son on your desk?"

"Yes, that's my son, Teddy."

"Did the morning sickness last all day?"

Sophia smiled as she sat down in her armchair. "Yes, it did. I've always felt the term morning sickness was a misnomer. If you need to use the bathroom at any time, just let me know."

Lorraine sat back, her hands still on her abdomen. "I think I'm okay for now."

"You look well otherwise. How far along are you?"

"I've been so upset about Conrad that I didn't notice I missed my period. The gynecologist said it'll be seven weeks next week."

"Any idea whose child it could be?"

Lorraine's face colored. "If you're asking if the child could be one of the men that I slept with at Conrad's insistence, I'm thinking that is highly unlikely, because we used protection."

"And Conrad?"

Lorraine shook her head, tears springing to her eyes. Sophia handed her a box of tissues.

"I have no idea why we didn't use protection. I've been so rash and stupid with all of this." She dabbed tears from her eyes.

"As I may have mentioned, rational thought doesn't usually go hand-in-hand with past life influenced experiences," said Sophia. "The decisions are often irrational and impulsive."

Lorraine balled up the tissue in her hands. "That sums up this debacle perfectly." Her eyes clouded. "What am I going to do?"

"First of all, you're going to calm down for your and the baby's sake. And then I must ask you. Do you wish to keep the baby?"

Lorraine sat up and nodded vigorously. "Even if the baby is Conrad's, I want to keep him." She rubbed her belly. "I only just found out that I'm pregnant, but I've got this strong feeling—maybe it's a maternal instinct—that the baby is a he."

Sophia let out a breath she didn't realize she was holding. "Well, that makes all of this much easier."

Lorraine raised her eyebrows. "It does?"

"As long as you love your child and want to keep him safe, there's nothing that you as a mother can't or won't do for him."

Lorraine's expression became hopeful. "Do you really think so, Dr. Strand?"

Sophia didn't usually share personal details with clients, but in this instance she felt the occasion warranted it. "I was a young mother. My son's father died in an IED blast in Afghanistan. Though I raised him as a single mother, he has thrived. So even if things don't work out for you with Stan, which I hope they do, I can tell you from personal experience that you'll be fine."

Lorraine sat up straighter. "Thank you for sharing that, Dr. Strand. That really helps." Her phone buzzed from within the depths of her purse. She dug around in her bag. "That's probably Conrad again. I'm sorry, I thought I shut it off." When she found the phone and looked at the screen, she grimaced. "He does this. Screaming at me, and then apologizing. Now he's saying he's sorry, and that he wants to meet tonight to make up." She shut off the phone and threw it in her purse. "I'm going to keep it off."

"I think that's a good idea," said Sophia. "Ready to regress now?"

Lorraine relaxed back on the couch. "I am totally ready, Dr. Strand. I trust you."

Sophia stopped short for a moment at Lorraine's words. She was finding that trust was a big part of the past life regression method. Even more so than regular, traditional therapy. She set her phone to play the sound of light rain and began.

When Lorraine walked through the purple door, she didn't know what to expect, but what she saw surprised her. It was night, and she and a man who looked like Stan were in bed, but it wasn't their bedroom. He lay beside her sleeping, his breathing soft and steady. She glanced around at her surroundings. They were in a small, simply furnished room. The curtain on a window stirred, and she heard a car's tires crackle on the asphalt as it drove by outside. It must have been summertime, as the air was warm. Against the wall was a small desk and wooden chair. She stifled a gasp when she saw what lay strung over the chair—a policeman's uniform.

"You're awake," he murmured then, his breath smelling faintly of mint. "Insomnia again?"

Unsure of what to say, she replied, "I guess."

"You're safe, Evelyn. He's in jail and not getting out anytime soon. And even when he does, I'll never let anything happen to you."

Lorraine was just beginning to feel a calm settle over her when suddenly things shifted, and she found herself running, barefoot, in a dark alley. She stepped on something that burned and tore at her foot but she kept running, even as she slipped on blood. She heard a sound behind her, and that only made her run even faster. Suddenly, a sharp pain tore through her abdomen and slammed the back of her spine, but she resisted the urge to slow down. She knew that stopping wasn't an option if she wanted to live.

Chapter 10

When Sophia saw Lorraine become agitated, she decided she better bring her back.

"Lorraine," she said softly, "I want you to return to the here and now. You will remember what you've seen, but it's time to come back to 2021. Follow my voice toward the purple door. The closer you come to the door, the further away from the past you will be. I'm going to count back from twenty now."

Lorraine had started to hyperventilate and sweat, so Sophia did the countdown more quickly than usual. "Twenty, nineteen, eighteen, seventeen, you can see the purple door coming closer, sixteen, fifteen, fourteen, thirteen, twelve, eleven, ten, nine, eight, seven, keep going, six, five, four, three, two, one. Open the purple door and step back into the present. You're now safe in Orange, California in 2021."

Lorraine's eyes remained firmly closed, and her skin had a gray cast to it that alarmed Sophia. But then slowly, she opened her eyes and turned to meet Sophia's gaze. She stared at her without speaking for a few moments, and then said, "I was with him."

"Conrad?"

She shook her head and motioned to sit up.

"Take your time getting up." Sophia cautioned her.

Lorraine slowly sat up and leaned back against the couch. "At first, I was with Stan. I think we were in his house. But he was Officer Pete. We were in bed together. He was sleeping, but he woke up and said something interesting to me."

"What was that?" asked Sophia.

"That I was safe because he was in jail, and that he, Officer Pete, would always protect me."

"How did that make you feel?" asked Sophia.

Lorraine instinctively brought her hands to her chest. "It reminded me of the early days with Stan. He made me feel so protected, so loved."

"It's not that way anymore?"

Lorraine sighed. "It's a funny thing when a man protects you. At first, it feels so wonderful—to know that you have a knight in shining armor. But then it becomes, I don't know, stifling."

Sophia nodded slowly. "I can see how that could become the case. Did anything else happen that you remember? Toward the end of your regression, I decided to bring you back, because you became agitated. You even started sweating."

Lorraine looked down at her feet. "At first, I was in the room with Officer Pete, and he was holding me, but then all of the sudden I was running through an alley. I think I stepped on a piece of glass, because my foot started bleeding. But I had to keep running because someone was chasing me."

"Do you remember anything else about what happened?"

"Yes, there was horrible pain in my belly, but I kept running. Do you think the running happened after that time in bed with Officer Pete?"

"Regressions are tricky that way. They don't necessarily come in chronological order. You often have to piece them together like a jigsaw puzzle."

"That makes sense," said Lorraine. "It's so odd how you feel like you're really there during the regression. It can be frightening sometimes. Like not knowing who was chasing me."

Sophia glanced at her phone to see that their session would soon be over. "Just remind yourself that was then and this is now. The past is over, and you're safe."

Lorraine screwed up her face and laughed harshly. "Am I, really? I have no idea what Conrad is going to do next. For all I know, he has already told Stan about us."

"I highly doubt it," said Sophia. "Conrad is using the threat of telling Stan to keep you in line. If he tells him, he doesn't have anything to hold over you. Unless he knows about the pregnancy."

"Oh, god, no!" exclaimed Lorraine. "And I'm not going to tell him. I'm not even going to tell Stan yet."

"Well, you still have some time. For now, I would strongly suggest keeping your distance from Conrad until we untangle what occurred all those years ago."

"Today is my and Stan's anniversary, like I mentioned to you. I'm thinking about surprising him with an impromptu getaway tonight. We have a cabin in Lake Arrowhead."

"That sounds like a great idea," said Sophia. "Getting away will give you a fresh perspective and time to just be together."

Sophia's phone pinged to mark the end of the session, and Lorraine picked up her purse. "Even though I have no idea what happened all those years ago, I feel better somehow. I think it's because Stan and I have been together before, and obviously been happy. I know we can do it again."

"That's a wonderful way to look at it," said Sophia as they both stood. "I'll see you for another session Monday morning at the same time."

After Sophia walked Lorraine out and returned to her office, she picked up her phone and went to her desk. She got out the file on Lorraine and was about to listen to the recording, but the thought of hearing Conrad again sent a chill through her. This time, she would make notes without listening to it.

Sophia arrived in Laguna Beach a little past noon and was lucky to find a parking spot. Though it was cold and blustery on the coast, there were still a lot of people about, including some sunbathers. Sophia was always amazed when people swam in the winter months here. True, it was Southern California, and the sun was shining, but the Pacific Ocean was extra chilly this time of year.

She was meeting her grandmother and Teddy at a restaurant across from the main beach. As she opened her car door, the caw of seagulls and salty air greeted her. She was about to get out when an image flashed through her mind. She and Phillip on a sailboat—the sea crashing around them. He struggled to secure the sail as the vessel rocked wildly back and forth. "Take ahold," he cried out, reaching out to grab her by the wrist and pull her to him. He wrapped his strong arms around her as the boat continued to nearly capsize with each ferocious wave as they clung to the mast, their feet slipping on the deck. The vision flashed forward then, and she saw them standing on deck, the storm having passed, flotsam bobbing in the water around them. Phillip laughed. "What a mess we've got, but we're still alive."

Her phone buzzed then and she pulled it out to see a message from Teddy. *We're at the restaurant. You on your way?* She replied that she had just parked and hurried out of the car. As she made her way to the restaurant, she thought about how since she'd been doing the past life regression work, she seemed to have opened a direct line to her own past lives with Phillip. At times, she felt as if she were walking around in an altered universe, and it was a bit unsettling.

When she walked into the restaurant, she spotted them sandwiched in a booth toward the back and waved as she approached.

"You made it," said her grandmother. "I hope your session went well?"

Sophia shrugged out of her sweater, then sat down and put it on her lap. "It did. I think she'll be okay for the rest of the weekend."

"Splendid," said her grandmother, handing her a menu. "Quick, pick what you want, so we can eat."

"I hope you haven't been waiting long," said Sophia as she opened the menu.

"Only forever," said Teddy. "And Grandma wouldn't let me order without you."

Sophia closed the menu. "I know what I want. A burger and fries and a strawberry shake."

"See!" said Teddy. "I knew what you were going to order, Mom. You always order the same thing."

After the waitress took their orders, her grandmother asked, "So, when will I be meeting Professor Kirten?"

Sophia laughed. "Before you were scolding me for setting you up, and now you're asking when you'll be meeting him. It just so happens that we're having a dinner party tomorrow evening. I invited Cathy and Chuck, and I spoke with Professor Kirten the other day, and he said he could come. Teddy, you can ask Cerise if she's available."

"You're going to really like Professor Kirten," said Teddy. "He's really cool, for an o—." Teddy stopped talking and blushed.

"I think you were going to say for an old guy," said her grandmother.

Teddy stuffed several French fries into his mouth, making speaking nearly impossible.

Her grandmother wasn't about to let him off the hook, though. "It's okay, we will wait until your mouth is empty."

Resigned to the inevitable, Teddy finished chewing and swallowed, then reached for his Coke and took a drink before replying. "That's what I was going to say, but I meant no disrespect."

"I know you didn't, dear. I can only hope that I am as cool as he is."

Sophia held back a giggle at the look of expectation on her grandmother's face as she waited for Teddy's reply.

"You're totally cool, Grandma," Teddy assured her. "The coolest."

After a filling lunch, they bundled up and took a walk along the water. Sophia was careful not to get her feet wet, but Teddy took off his shoes and ran in the surf, whooping as the cold water hit his legs.

"Our boy looks happy," said her grandmother as they watched him play chicken with the waves.

Sophia smiled to see Teddy so light and happy. "He does."

They walked in silence for a time, and then her grandmother said, "You seem quiet."

"I had another one of my awake visions of Phillip and me. It must have been brought on by being here at the beach. We were on a sailboat and got caught in a cyclone."

Her grandmother glanced at her profile, then reached down and picked up a conch shell, admiring it as they walked. "And this vision, did it have a happy ending?"

"It did. We both held onto the mast and weathered the storm. We were still on the boat once things had calmed down, though it was pretty battered."

Her grandmother looked up at the sun, then back down at the conch shell. "And you can't help but wonder when you have visions like that why you and Phillip couldn't have had such an outcome in this lifetime?"

"Exactly."

"While I can't tell you everything, I can tell you what I've told you before. You were meant to part in this lifetime in the physical sense, but as you know you are never separated in the spiritual sense."

Up ahead, Teddy had stopped to make a sandcastle. Sophia turned to face her grandmother. "That's exactly what Phillip has told me during regressions when we've spoken about this, and to a certain extent, I do understand. I would probably not be doing the regressions with clients if I hadn't lost him. But...," she trailed off.

Her grandmother placed a hand on Sophia's arm. "But you are human, and the feeling of Phillip in your arms—the physical feeling—is something you crave. That's perfectly natural."

Sophia felt tears well up in her throat, and she tried to swallow them down. "What should I do, Grandmother?"

Her grandmother's eyes filled with compassion. "You continue to do what you are doing—being the best mother to Teddy, and therapist for your patients. And you continue to love Phillip, because he will always be a part of you." She tipped Sophia's face up with a forefinger to her chin. "And when it is time, and I believe that time will come sooner than you realize, you open yourself up to another."

Sophia shook her head slightly as if to argue the point. "I don't know, Grandmother. I doubt I will ever find someone who can measure up. You didn't with Grandfather, did you?"

"My situation was different. I lost your grandfather after twenty-five years of marriage. You and Phillip were only together for a short time. You're still young."

"But how will I ever find someone who is..." Sophia stopped talking and swallowed.

"Good enough?" her grandmother asked. "Are you referring to good enough for you, or good enough for Phillip?"

The question surprised Sophia.

"I believe that what is stopping you is the fear that Phillip will never agree to you and another man. That he will be more exacting about who you choose than you." Her grandmother waited while Sophia processed her statement.

Finally, Sophia nodded. "I think you might have something there."

"Well, I'll tell you right now that is something you needn't worry about. All Phillip wants is for you to be happy. So, when the right person comes along. And he will. I guarantee you he will give you a green light. And if you are worried that at that point Phillip will leave you, don't. He will always be here for you and Teddy."

Sophia brushed stray tears from her eyes with cold fingers as Teddy motioned for them to come help. "I truly don't know what I would do without your wise counsel."

Her grandmother put her arm around Sophia as they headed for Teddy. "Thankfully that is not something you have to find out."

Chapter 12

They returned to Orange in the late afternoon and decided to stop at a coffee shop near Sophia's condo. When they sat down with their beverages, Sophia was delighted when who should walk into the shop but Professor Kirten.

She waved to him as he entered, but failed to catch his eye.

"Excuse me for a moment. Professor Kirten just came in, and I want to invite him to our table, if he'll be staying." She smiled when, out of the corner of her eye, she saw her grandmother surreptitiously adjust the purple scarf she was wearing.

Sophia approached Professor Kirten, now standing in line. He wore a red and black striped cardigan vest and black slacks, his gray hair tucked under his familiar beret.

"Why, Sophia, how delightful to see you here," he said, beaming. "You look refreshed. I don't often see you out of your office togs, as they say."

Sophia glanced down at the yoga pants and long-sleeved shirt she had changed into at the office before heading to Laguna. "My grandmother and Teddy and I just spent some time at the beach," she said. "As a matter of fact, my grandmother is here now. I'd love to introduce you to her."

"Oh, my, what fortunate timing," said Professor Kirten. "And to think I almost walked past but the aroma of coffee pulled me in." He glanced over at Teddy and her grandmother, who had their heads together.

"Well, I'm glad you stopped," said Sophia, now eyeing some chocolate brownies in the display case.

"That's the beauty of retirement," he said. "Nowadays, I have time to not only stop and smell the coffee, but I can also taste it. Although, I do admit I've been spending more time at the college lately preparing for my Philosophy of Religion class that I'll be teaching next semester."

"How is the class shaping up?" asked Sophia.

"Swimmingly," he said as the barista asked for his order. He peered at the name tag on her shirt. "Jessica, I hope the day is treating you well. I'd like an Earl Grey tea and one of those scrumptious looking blueberry muffins." He turned to Sophia. "Would you like something?"

"I was thinking about splitting a couple of brownies with Teddy and my grandmother, but I can get them."

"Nonsense. Two brownies for the young lady, and put it on my tab." Then he pulled out his wallet and slipped his credit card into the machine.

The cashier slid the pastries into brown paper bags and handed them to Professor Kirten, then put a tea bag into a cup and poured hot water over it.

As they turned to make their way to the table where Teddy and her grandmother sat, Sophia noted that he didn't have the cane she'd seen him with on recent occasions. "You don't have your cane today."

"Turns out that I may be able to resolve all of this with some simple physical therapy, rather than hip surgery."

Teddy motioned to stand when they walked up, but Professor Kirten put out a hand and said, "No, need, Theodore." Then he turned to her grandmother. "This must be your grandmother. Lovely to meet you. Your granddaughter has painted a wonderful picture of you, and I see that she wasn't exaggerating."

Her grandmother smiled. "Please call me Ophelia. And it is very nice to meet you. Sophia has many good things to say about you. Won't you sit with us?"

"I would be delighted." He took a seat at the table. "I understand you are from Greece. That is a country I've always wanted to experience."

"It's a great place to visit," said Teddy. "My mom and I go once every year or so."

Sophia's phone vibrated then, and she reached into her purse to pull it out. A message from Lorraine: *Hi, Dr. Strand. I just wanted to let you know that everything is okay for the moment. Stan doesn't know anything, and he's excited about our anniversary trip. We're heading out in a few minutes. I'll see you next week.*

Sophia put her phone away. "I think I just heard my name mentioned."

"I was just explaining to the professor how you used to perform therapy sessions for your Barbie dolls," said her grandmother.

"Oh, do call me by my given name, which is Randall," said Professor Kirten. "Now about those Barbie dolls. They must have been very well adjusted."

Sophia laughed. "It was mostly marriage counseling sessions between Barbie and Ken. I'm not sure how effective the sessions were, though."

They continued chatting for the next hour until they all agreed to part ways and resume the fun the next night at Sophia's for dinner.

"What do you think of Professor Kirten?" Teddy asked as they headed to the car.

"I think he is charming, highly intelligent, and a great conversationalist. He also has a wry sense of humor," said her grandmother.

"He must really like you," said Teddy. "He only told me I could call him Randall after knowing him for years."

Her grandmother pulled open the car door and got in. "Well, we are contemporaries. It would be silly for us to be overly formal." She looked over at Sophia, who was inserting the key in the ignition. "I see that grin about to erupt. Out with it."

Sophia shrugged her shoulders. "I was just thinking that it looks like I was right. You and Professor, I mean, Randall, have hit it off."

Her grandmother smiled, then yawned. "The jet lag still seems to be hounding me. If you both don't mind, I'll turn in early tonight."

"Good idea," said Teddy. "You want to be fresh for your date with Professor Kirten tomorrow night."

"Teddy!" cried Sophia. Then they all burst out laughing.

Chapter 13

That evening after her grandmother had gone to bed and Teddy holed himself up in the den to talk to Cerise, Sophia cleaned up the dinner dishes and turned on the dishwasher. Then she made herself a cup of herbal tea and took it to the living room, where she sat on the sofa and heaved a sigh of contentment. As she relaxed, the hum of the dishwasher in the background, she felt her eyes grow heavy, and she laid her head back.

Sophia found herself walking on a deserted country road, a fluttery noise surrounding her, like blades of grass shifting in the wind, but the air was still. She stopped to survey the land and saw that the sound came from the locusts eating everything green in their path. She wore a pair of worn shoes, her big toe pushing up through the cracked leather. Her gingham dress had been darned in several areas. She held a basket in her hands and gasped to see that it was empty. The crabapples she'd picked from the tree in the nearby field were missing. She looked behind her at the road, hoping to see them scattered along the path she'd taken, but all she saw was dusty dirt. Had she left them by the tree? How could she be so careless.

She ran back to the field, relieved to find the apples in a pile on the ground next to the now bare tree. She rushed to pick them up, locusts hopping in her path. But when she got to the apples, a hand shot out suddenly to take one. A boy put the fruit in his mouth as mischief danced in his eyes.

"Give me back my apple," she shrieked, reaching to snatch it from his mouth.

But he stepped back several paces and took a deep bite, then nodded to the apples still on the ground. "The locusts just about ate them, but I saved them for you."

It was then that she recognized him. Phillip as a boy.

"What are you doing here," she stammered as she picked up the rest of the apples.

"I should be asking you that," said the boy. "This is my family's land. Those are my family's apples."

Sophia held the basket to her, feeling her heart pounding in her chest. "But we need the apples for my baby sister, Millie."

"I suppose you can take them," he said, then took another bite of apple. "We'll all be dead before long, anyway, with no food. Your sister Millie included."

"Don't say that!" cried Sophia. "You're a nasty boy."

"I ain't no boy. I'm practically a man. I'm thirteen," he replied. "My name is John. Me and my family, we're heading west away from the locusts and the dusty land. You should come with us."

"I can't just come with you," cried Sophia, backing away from him. "I don't know you."

"Sure, you know me," he said. "You've always known me."

As Sophia turned and began to run away from the boy, she heard him shout after her, "Hey come back!" But when she turned, he was lost in a swarm of locusts, grown thicker now and making it hard to see as she made her way home. Through the flying insects she ran, holding tight to the basket of apples. When she came to the cabin, she yanked the door open and stepped inside quickly, slamming it behind her. She stood with her back against the door panting until she caught her breath. Once her breathing slowed, she heard a soft mewing sound coming from a cradle next to the potbelly stove. She set the apples on the floor and went over to find a baby lying there, her fist in her mouth, her eyes closed.

"She's right pretty when she sleeps," said a voice behind her.

Sophia would know that voice anywhere. "Grandmother?" she said as she spun around to see a woman wearing a gingham dress like Sophia's. She looked to be in her early thirties and had a bandana covering her dark hair.

"What's the talk about your grandmother?" said the woman, putting her hands on her hips. "Your grandmother is long dead and buried, bless her soul. Now watch your sister while mama makes her some applesauce."

The woman went into a small, makeshift kitchen in the one-room cabin and began pulling the apples out of the basket and admiring them. "You done good, girl," she said. "Now your sister got something to eat 'sides my milk while we wait for your Pa to come back from hunting. Where'd you find these?"

"The land to the north of us. I met the boy who lives there."

The woman gave her a funny look. "You talking about the Kettleman's land?"

"I reckon so," said Sophia.

Her mother stopped cutting. "What did this boy look like?"

"He was tall and thin and wore overalls. He had light colored hair and said his name was John and that he was thirteen years old. He and his family are going west, and he said we should go with them."

Her mother resumed cutting the apples. "Them locusts done got to your head, child. The Kettleman's only son died last year. They left their land soon after. I'm surprised you found apples there. From what I heard, the townsfolk picked everything bare."

"But I know I saw him," said Sophia.

"Like I done told you, them locusts got to your head."

Sophia awoke to a quiet house and glanced at the clock on the wall. She'd been asleep for several hours. As she sat up and reached for her now cold tea, she was jolted by the memory of her dream. She'd been with her grandmother, but her grandmother was her mother. And she'd been talking to Phillip's ghost.

Chapter 14

The next morning, Sophia jumped out of bed, eager to tell her grandmother about the dream from the night before. Instead, she found a note in Teddy's scrawl, *Grandmother and I went on a walk. There's coffee, and we made oat muffins. We'll be back soon.*

She picked a still warm muffin off a plate, then poured a cup of coffee and sat down at the island to read the notes she'd made the night before about the dream.

"You're drinking your coffee black nowadays?" asked Phillip.

She slammed the notebook down, her heart slip-slapping around in her chest. "You startled me."

"My apologies, love, but you were lost in thought."

She looked down at the notebook, then back at Phillip's flickering image. "It appears that this lifetime isn't the only one where you've communicated with me beyond the grave."

"No, it isn't."

Just then the front door opened and Sophia heard Teddy's voice.

"You're up, little love," said her grandmother when they both walked in, her eyes going to the notebook in Sophia's hands. "Getting some work done?"

"Not exactly. I had some questions for you."

"I'm going to take a quick shower," said Teddy.

When they were alone, her grandmother faced Sophia, her face lined with concern. "What is it?"

Sophia put her head in her hands and sighed as her grandmother took a seat across from her. "How do you do this day in and day out, Grandmother?"

"I think you are referring to connecting with the dead?"

"Yes. It's honestly so exhausting. This back and forth and push and pull. Do you sometimes wish you didn't have the gift?"

Her grandmother glanced at the notebook clasped in Sophia's hands. "Does this have something to do with what you have written there? Is this about Phillip again?"

Sophia sighed. "That is the operative word. Again, and again, and again, and again. Just how many times have I known him in other lifetimes?"

Her grandmother smiled and reached over and pulled a piece off the muffin that Sophia had yet to eat and popped it in her mouth. "That's difficult to say, but many. These are quite good, aren't they? You've taught Teddy well in the kitchen."

"Speaking of Teddy. I've probably known him in many lifetimes. And you. We've known each other countless times, haven't we?"

Her grandmother looked amused. "Of course. Good thing we get along so well."

"I find it annoying that you can laugh about this," said Sophia, feeling incredibly frustrated for reasons she couldn't quite pinpoint.

"What would you have me do, cry? And what is so terrible about it? Tell me, what is in that notebook of yours?"

Sophia felt so overcome with unidentified emotions that she didn't think she could speak. Instead, she pushed the notebook to her grandmother. "Go ahead. Read all about it."

When she had finished reading, she closed the notebook and patted it. Sophia, who expected her grandmother to comment on how odd the dream had been, instead shocked her by simply saying, "I remember that lifetime."

At her reply, Sophia suddenly became keenly aware of the clock ticking on the wall. It was as if time had suspended, and they might flip to another lifetime that she didn't recognize. Finally, when the silence became nearly unbearable, she asked, "And Millie. Who was Millie?"

Her grandmother waited, as if daring Sophia to remember.

Sophia shot out the first name that flashed through her mind. "Cerise?"

At that moment, Teddy came walking into the room, running a towel through his thick hair. "What about Cerise?" He looked from his mother to his great grandmother.

Sophia tapped the pen on the notebook. "We were just discussing who is coming to dinner tonight. You did invite Cerise, didn't you?"

Teddy tipped his head to one side. "Mom, I was right there when you invited her. Remember? She's also going to be here in a little while to go to the Bowers Museum and then lunch."

"Oh, that's right. Good, I'm glad she's coming."

Teddy stood there with a confused expression on his face. "I feel like I'm missing something."

"You're not missing anything," Sophia assured him. "Go finish getting ready."

After Teddy left the room, her grandmother said, "It might be a good idea for you to tell him."

The undefined irritation surged through Sophia once again. "Tell him what? That I talk to his dead father? Or that we've all known each other in other lifetimes?"

Her grandmother shrugged her shoulders. "All of it."

Sophia let out a big breath, then reminded herself what she would tell a client. If there is something that is bothering you, and you feel like lashing out in frustration, examine what is really going on—what is the underlying cause?

"I can see the wheels turning," said her grandmother. "Care to share?"

Sophia pushed her hair back and stared at the table for a moment, then said, "I'm sorry if I've been short with you. I'm trying to understand why all of this is frustrating and even infuriating me."

"Would you care for my input?"

"It seems that I should be old enough to figure this out on my own.

Not to mention that I'm a therapist and have had schooling on this subject." Sophia took a sip of her now cold coffee and grimaced.

"There is nothing wrong with seeking counsel, even though you are the counselor."

"You don't."

Her grandmother raised an eyebrow. "How do you know that?"

"This is something I've never heard about. Who do you seek counsel from?"

Her grandmother seemed to consider for a moment. "He was and still is my mentor. His name is Horatio."

"Why have I not heard about him?"

"He hasn't come up."

"Tell me about him. When did you meet him?"

"I first met him when I was young in my village. He was a visiting philosophy professor from Spain at the time. He worked with my father at the University of Athens."

Sophia shook her head as if to clear it. "I'm confused. He worked with your father? Great Grandfather died many years ago. This Horatio must be very old."

Her grandmother smiled. "He was nearly one hundred when he passed."

"Oh, so he was your mentor. Who do you talk to now?"

"Horatio," her grandmother said simply.

It took Sophia a few moments to understand what her grandmother had just told her. "You mean you talk to him from the other side now?"

"I do, yes."

Sophia found this fascinating. "How do you communicate with him?"

Her grandmother took a sip of coffee. "Much like you communicate with Phillip. Sometimes he simply comes to me when he wishes to give me a message. At other times, I ask for answers to my inquiries."

"And he answers you?"

Her grandmother nodded. "He does."

"You ask a question, and he shows up and answers you?"

"Often, yes, but he also answers me in dreams, and sometimes I'm compelled to write a message down, which will turn out to be my answer."

Sophia stood and went to the microwave to reheat her coffee, mulling over what her grandmother had just said. "Does that mean I could ask Phillip questions? I know I have asked him questions about him and me, but are you saying I could ask him questions about other things in order to get his perspective from the other side?"

"Bingo," said her grandmother, who held out her cup to Sophia. "Could you reheat my coffee as well?"

Sophia took her cup and put it in the microwave when the doorbell rang. "That must be Cerise. I better get dressed."

"Go," said her grandmother. "I can get my coffee. Don't forget to eat your muffin."

Sophia grabbed her muffin and took that and her coffee to her room, where she set them down on the table next to the window and sat down. As the sound of Teddy and Cerise's voices floated by in the hallway, Sophia closed her eyes and decided to put her grandmother's information to the test. "Phillip," she whispered. "Can you and will you answer my questions when I need assistance?"

She jumped when an answer came back immediately. "I will, my love." She opened her eyes and glanced around the room but saw no one. Then she heard, "You don't have to see me to hear me."

"But I like to see you."

"I materialize when I can, but it's not always possible from here. What is your burning question?"

Sophia thought about what she wanted to know and struggled to put it into words. "I guess my main question at the moment is why I'm feeling so irritable about the mention of you. That doesn't sound so good when I say it out loud."

Phillip laughed. "The good news is that from here we really can't get our feelings hurt. At least not too much. But to answer your question, I think you know the answer. You are angry because I'm not there in the flesh."

Sophia sighed. "I thought I had worked past that years ago, but you're saying I haven't?"

Silence.

In the bathroom, she washed her face and brushed her teeth, thinking how grief and loss were such a complex terrain. She looked in the mirror at herself, searching for clues as to how the loss of Phillip may have affected her physically. Did it show in her eyes?

A knock on her bedroom door brought her back to the present. "Mom, you about ready? It'd be good to get to the museum soon, so we don't miss our lunch reservation after."

Sophia was still not dressed. "I'll be out in five minutes!" She quickly applied some makeup and brushed through her hair, then pulled on a sweater and slacks. As she left her room, Phillip whispered in her ear, "And we're off."

When they returned from the museum, Sophia's phone rang. She went out onto the balcony to answer. "This is Dr. Strand."

"I'm so glad I got you," cried Lorraine.

"What's going on?"

"I don't know what to do. I think he might know."

"Who knows what?"

"Stan. I think he may know about Conrad and me."

"What happened? And are you in a safe place to talk?"

"I'm in the car in front of a grocery store up in Lake Arrowhead. Stan is in the store right now picking up some supplies for tonight. I told him I'd be right in, so I don't have much time."

"What happened to make you think that he knows?"

"He's acting a little odd. And he mentioned Conrad a few times."

"That's all?"

"Yes, but he's unusually quiet."

"He could have something else on his mind. Did you ask him?"

"God no, what if he says he knows about me and Conrad."

"Lorraine, be honest with me. Do you feel unsafe right now?"

She hesitated for a moment but then assured Lorraine, "I don't think Stan would ever hurt me, if that's what you're asking. Conrad on the other hand."

"But Conrad isn't there."

"No."

"I'm assuming you're calling me for some moral support and advice?"

"Yes. What should I do? Tell Stan about the pregnancy?"

"Do you think the child is his?"

"That's the problem. I don't know. The gynecologist said I need to wait until next week to take a blood test that will check for paternity."

"Are you continuing to avoid speaking with Conrad?"

"Yes. I haven't turned on the phone he gave me since I turned it off in your office."

"That's really the best you can do for now. My advice would be to act as normally as possible and enjoy this anniversary with Stan. A remote cabin is not an advisable place to tell your husband that you haven't been faithful and could be carrying another man's child. And if at any point you feel like you are in danger, then call the authorities or get to safety."

Lorraine heaved a sigh. "That's good advice. I'm going to go into the store before he gets suspicious. Thanks for being there, Dr. Strand. I don't know what I'd do without you."

Sophia went back inside to see that she only had three hours until that night's dinner party. She had to work quickly to figure out what to serve. She checked the refrigerator to see that there wasn't much there. Then she thought of the perfect recipe.

"I'm going to the store to get some things for dinner," she told Teddy, who had come into the kitchen for a drink of water.

"What are we having?"

"Chicken Kiev. You can help me make it when I get back."

Twenty minutes later, Sophia was at Albertsons standing in front of the breadcrumbs. She reached for a box and dropped it in her cart, then turned quickly and crashed into another cart.

"I'm so sorry!" she exclaimed to the startled man on the other side of the cart.

He recovered quickly and smiled. "Not to worry. Breadcrumbs still intact." Then he tipped his head and looked at her closely. "Do we know one another?"

He was tall and fit, with black hair pulled into a ponytail and had an easy way about himself. He wore a brown jacket and jeans, and flip flops, and Sophia spotted a small earring in one ear.

"I'm not sure," said Sophia. "Are you from around here?"

"Not originally, but I've lived in Orange since the nineties. Perhaps I know you from Chapman? Are you an instructor there?"

"I'm an alum. Are you an instructor?"

"Yes, I teach physics and chemistry."

Sophia felt as if her heart stopped and started for a moment. "You've been at Chapman since the nineties? Perhaps you knew my late husband, Phillip?"

"I knew Phillip well. We worked together. You're Sophia, aren't you? Phillip talked about you all the time."

Sophia felt tongue-tied suddenly at this man knowing her by name. "I am," she finally managed to reply. "May I ask your name?"

"It's Ryan Collins. I can't tell you how nice it is to finally meet you. I saw you at Phillip's funeral and thought about introducing myself, but I didn't want to intrude."

When Sophia didn't reply, he said, "I'm sorry, I tend to say the darndest things. I shouldn't have mentioned your husband's funeral. Forgive me."

Finally finding her voice, Sophia spoke up, "I'm sorry, I didn't mean to be rude. It's not every day that I meet a colleague of Phillip's."

"Now that we've both been awkward, it's very nice to meet you, Sophia." Ryan reached out his hand and took hers. His grasp felt warm and reassuring. "Do you live nearby?"

"Yes, I do. You?"

"I live in Old Towne in an old fixer upper. An 1890 Craftsman. It's actually in pretty good shape nowadays. It should be, I've been working on it for a decade now."

"It must be lovely," said Sophia. "Well, I better be moving along. I have company to cook for tonight."

"I'll let you go then," he said. "Again, very nice to finally meet you."

When Sophia got to the end of the aisle, she peeked back to see Ryan pulling a can from the shelves. Something about his profile seemed familiar.

On her way home, Sophia decided to file away her unexpected meeting with Phillip's former colleague for now. The experience had unnerved and excited her all at the same time, and she would need some quiet time to process it.

"Do you want me to look up a recipe for Chicken Kiev on my phone?" asked Teddy when they were in the kitchen ready to cook.

"That won't be necessary. I've got something special to show you," said Sophia. She went into the living room and pulled a photo album out of the entertainment center.

"No offense, Mom, but is this really a good time to stroll down memory lane? Everybody is going to be here in a couple of hours."

Sophia sat on the sofa and thumbed to the page she sought. "Humor me and come look at something."

Teddy complied and sat down next to Sophia to look at a photo in the album. "That's Dad with you in the kitchen. Is that Chicken Kiev?"

"It is," said Sophia. "Your father came over one night with all the ingredients, and we made it together. Now you and I can make it for tonight." She flipped to the end of the album and pulled a slip of paper out of the back pocket and handed it to Teddy.

"It's a recipe for Chicken Kiev. Is it Dad's?"

Sophia laughed. "From what I remember, he found the recipe in a woman's magazine at the grocery store and jotted it down while he stood in line."

In addition to the main dish, they made roasted potatoes and tossed a salad. Sophia had hoped to make an apple cobbler for dessert, but they ran out of time. The ice cream in the freezer would have to suffice.

"I'm going to get dressed. Can you watch the oven?"

"Sure. And, Mom, thanks. It was really cool to make something that you and Dad made together." He held the recipe in his hands.

"You're welcome, honey. And if you want to keep the recipe, you can."

Teddy looked at the paper lined with fold marks. "Thanks, I'd like that."

Chapter 16

As the scent of Chicken Kiev wafted throughout the condo, Sophia emerged from her bedroom to find her grandmother in the living room talking with Cerise.

"I was just telling Cerise what it's like to live in Greece. She has always wanted to visit," said her grandmother.

"Well, then, you'll have to come with us when we go," said Sophia.

Cerise's face lit up. "Really? Oh, I'd love that."

The doorbell rang just then, and Sophia excused herself. On the doorstep, stood Cathy and Chuck. Her sister-in-law handed her a bottle of wine.

"Thank you. I'm so glad you two could join us," said Sophia. "Come on in."

"Dinner smells amazing," said Cathy as they took off their jackets and Sophia hung them in the entryway closet.

"Everyone is in the living room. Would you both like some wine?"

"I'd love some," said Cathy, "but the big guy might want a beer."

"Whatever is easiest," said Chuck.

"I got your favorite IPA," she told him. "Go ahead in. I'll bring you your drinks."

After checking the chicken, she opened the wine and filled a wineglass, then grabbed a beer and uncapped it. Just as she entered the living room with the drinks, the doorbell rang.

Teddy jumped up. "That must be Professor Kirten. I'll get it."

Moments later, Professor Kirten walked in, Teddy behind him. Her son held up a box. "He read our minds and brought dessert."

"I hope that was okay," said the older man, dressed in black slacks, a crisp, bright yellow dress shirt, and a black bow tie that matched his signature black beret.

"That is more than okay. I was just telling Teddy how I wished we'd had time to make dessert, and you came to the rescue."

A broad smile covered the man's face. "Delightful to see all of you."

"Come, sit, Randall," said her grandmother, patting the sofa beside her. "Unless you need help in the kitchen, Sophia?"

"Teddy and I have it covered. You all just relax."

As they made their way to the kitchen, he whispered, "I think you were right. They seem to like each other."

Sophia had just set the pie on the counter when her cellphone buzzed. "Can you check the chicken and get it out if it's done? I need to get this call."

Sophia didn't even have a chance to get a word out before Lorraine wailed in her ear, "Dr. Strand, I don't know what to do."

"What's happening now?" she asked, glancing over to see that Teddy had removed the chicken. When he looked at her with questions in his eyes, she held up her fingers to indicate five minutes, then went down the hall to her bedroom. Once inside with the door closed, she sat on the edge of her bed and said in a firm voice, "Take several deep breaths. I can't help you if I can't understand you."

The woman gulped air for a few moments, then finally said, her voice a whimper, "I need help, Dr. Strand."

"That much is clear. Tell me what happened."

"I went back into the store earlier, and everything seemed okay. Stan and I bought food and went to the cabin. I had made a great dinner and was just putting it on the table when he came into the kitchen with a really weird look on his face."

When she didn't continue, Sophia prompted, "Go on."

Lorraine took a ragged breath. "It was then I noticed he had the phone Conrad gave me."

"Why on earth did you bring it with you?" asked Sophia.

"I didn't realize it was still in my purse. He was looking in there for some gum and found it."

"What did you say?"

"He wanted to know why I had another phone, and I told him I couldn't tell him, but that I'd tell him soon."

Sophia sighed. "Let me guess, that didn't go over well."

"Not at all. He had turned it on, but didn't know the password, of course, and demanded that I explain myself. I kept asking him to trust me, but he said that I'd been acting strange for months, and now he found a phone, and it was obvious to him what the phone was for, meaning that I'm having an affair. And if I wasn't going to explain myself, he was going to leave, so he did."

"Well, you can't blame him," said Sophia.

"But what do I do? Stan's now thinking the worst of me, and I'm here in Arrowhead without a car."

Teddy knocked several times and then stuck his head in and mouthed, "Dinner is ready."

"Hold on a second, Lorraine," she said, then asked Teddy, "Can you put it on the table, honey?"

Teddy nodded and shut the door.

"I'm back."

"I'm sorry, Dr. Strand. I know you have a life, and I keep interrupting you during off hours. I just feel so alone and confused, and I'm trying not to get too upset, because they say it's bad for the baby."

As she said this, Sophia flashed back to the early days of her pregnancy. "I know that it's hard to stay calm, but you're right, getting upset isn't good for the baby. Stan is angry right now, but he'll likely calm down, and then you can talk about it."

"But what on earth will I say?"

"First things first," said Sophia. "I want you to have some of that dinner you prepared, and then get some rest. Can you do that?"

"I'll try."

"Tomorrow is there someone who can come and pick you up?"

"I can always call Dahlia. She'll be back from vacation with Kevin by then."

"Okay, good." Sophia could hear plates clattering in the kitchen. "I've got to go now. You'll be okay. Every marriage has its ups and downs. Let me know if you need anything else."

Sophia waited for Lorraine's reply and was met with a screech.

"What is it?"

"Conrad must have been tracking the phone he gave me. Since Stan turned it on, he knows where I am, and he says he's on the way—that we have to talk. What do I do?"

Slivers of apprehension crept up Sophia's back. She had a very bad feeling about this.

"You need to leave immediately. Do you think you could get an Uber out of there?"

"I already tried before I called you, but there aren't any drivers right now available to make their way down the mountain. Dr. Strand, I'm a sitting duck."

"And you don't think that Stan would come back for you?"

"I've tried calling his phone multiple times. It just goes straight to voicemail."

Sophia considered suggesting Lorraine call the local authorities, but what would she tell them? That her boyfriend said he was coming to talk to her?

"It'll take me a couple of hours to drive there, but I'll come get you. I don't have a good feeling about you being alone with Conrad if he does show up."

"Oh, Dr. Strand, would you? I feel so alone and scared out here all by myself. If anything happened to this baby, I don't know what I would do."

"Give me the address of the cabin."

When she hung up, Sophia noticed that her hands were trembling. She took several deep breaths, then changed into jeans, a sweatshirt, and tennis shoes. When she entered the dining room where everyone was getting settled for dinner, her grandmother gave her a knowing look. "Is it work?"

"I'm so sorry to have to dash out, but, yes, it's a client."

"You know you don't have to do house calls," said Cathy.

"I know but the client is really in distress. It's a unique situation. I'll be back as soon as I can but it may not be until later."

"Go do what you must, dear," said Professor Kirten. "When duty calls, duty calls. Theodore is the perfect host."

"I've got it, Mom," agreed Teddy.

Her grandmother stood. "Let me walk you out."

When they got to the front door, she put her hands on Sophia's shoulders, concern in her eyes. "Are you certain about this? I sense that you're walking into some danger."

Sophia didn't bother to lie to her grandmother. "It is a potentially volatile situation, which is why I'm going. I'm hoping that if I get there in time, I can remove the client before anything happens and drop her at a hotel."

Her grandmother sighed. "If we didn't have the dinner party, I'd go with you. This is the past life client?"

Sophia nodded. "I'll be okay. I promise." Then she pecked her grandmother on the cheek and left the condo, praying that she was right.

Chapter 17

"What are you doing, little love?"

Sophia looked at her grandmother, clenching her jaw to fight back tears. She had torn up her bedroom and now sat amidst the mess, what she had been looking for in her hands. Her diary—its gilt edges glinting in the afternoon light. "I was looking for something," she said, wanting to flip to the pages she sought, yet on the other hand feeling like burning the entire journal.

Her grandmother leaned against the doorway, her expression somber. "And you found what you were looking for?"

Sophia closed her eyes to see visions of her and Phillip the night they had made love. The night her child had been conceived. She had come home and written in her diary about how beautiful her first time had been. Right now, she had a burning need to read what she had written. She closed her eyes to hold the torrent of tears that wanted to break free. "It's my diary," she said, her voice cracking.

Her grandmother came in and sat on the edge of the bed next to Sophia. "Diaries have a way of doing that."

Sophia's eyes burning still, she snapped them open. "Doing what?"

"Pulling us to the memories, while at the same time we wish to shy from them." She pulled a tissue out of her pocket and handed it to Sophia. "Is there a particular passage in the diary you are looking for?"

Sophia took the tissue and nodded. Though she'd known now for two weeks that she was pregnant, the news still seemed surreal. "The night the baby was conceived. We were at Joshua Tree under the stars."

"That must be a beautiful memory," said her grandmother.

Sophia's heart clutched. "I don't know if I can do this, Grandmother."

"What, have the baby, or raise the baby as a young mother?"

"Both. Maybe I should move to Greece with you."

Her grandmother was leaving tomorrow after staying with her since Phillip's death and funeral. She knelt on the floor in front of Sophia, then pushed hair out of her granddaughter's eyes and held her cheeks gently in the palms of her hands. "While I would love nothing more than to bring you back to Greece with me and watch that belly of yours grow, it is not a part of your destiny."

"But, how do you know that?" Sophia protested.

"I just know. You've made a home here with people who love you and depend on you. Though you've only just begun at the clinic, you already have clients, and you'll be helping many people as your practice develops. This loss has cut just as deep for Cathy, and she is going to need you more than ever. In fact, you'll need each other." Her grandmother put her hand on Sophia's stomach. "The little being inside of you will save you both. You'll see. It will all work out."

Sophia focused on the road and thought about Lorraine and her baby and how vulnerable she must be feeling. She glanced at her phone on the passenger seat. No texts or calls since she'd heard from her a half hour ago. Hopefully, she could hang on and remain calm until Sophia got there.

Sophia had been heading up the mountain for more than an hour. According to the GPS, she should arrive at the cabin soon. She slowed down as she entered the mountainside town of Lake Arrowhead. It was dark up here, with few streetlights, and the moon was just a sliver in the sky. The navigation system told her to take a right, and then she began traveling along a dark gravel road that went on for some distance. Finally, when she was told she'd arrived at her destination, Sophia made out a cabin on a hill at the end of long driveway. But the cabin was dark. Had she been taken to the wrong address? She drove up the drive and stopped the car in front of the house, shutting off the lights and lowering the driver's side window to listen. No sounds coming from outside, except for the car engine clinking as it settled. She picked up her cellphone and dialed Lorraine's number and waited. It rang for some time as Sophia's stomach began curdling with dread. Had Conrad beat her here and harmed Lorraine?

To her relief, Lorraine finally answered, her voice a whisper. "Hello?"

"It's me, Dr. Strand. I think I'm here at the cabin, but the house is dark. Did you turn off the lights?"

"Oh, thank god, you're here. Yes, I did turn them off. Someone was knocking on the door about fifteen minutes ago, but I didn't answer."

Sophia glanced around in the darkness and didn't see anyone. "It looks like whoever it was may have left. I'll come to the door now."

"Okay, I'm all ready to go."

Sophia got out of the car and shut the door quietly, then began walking to the front of the house but stopped and held her breath when she thought she heard a twig crack. After a few long moments of silence, she resumed hurrying up the path strewn with fallen pine needles. In the doorway stood Lorraine, holding a suitcase and purse. She glanced warily over Sophia's shoulder.

"I can't be sure," said Sophia in a low voice, "but I think we're clear. Let's get you to the car as quickly as possible."

Lorraine locked the door, then scurried along with Sophia to her car.

"It's unlocked," Sophia told her.

When Lorraine pulled open the passenger door and was about to get in, a voice sounded from the trees, "Lorraine."

"Get in!" cried Sophia, who jumped into the driver's seat and turned the key in the ignition, gunning the engine and backing up as soon as Lorraine's door had closed. There wasn't enough room to turn around, so she'd have to back down. As she did so, a man came running after them, waving his arms. He was big and muscular, his gait imposing.

"That's Conrad," Lorraine shrieked.

Panic zinged through Sophia as she continued backing up, doing her best to keep an eye on Conrad and the drive behind them.

When he rushed at the car and slammed his hands on the hood, Sophia yelled, "Hold on!" Then she floored the vehicle, flying backwards, Conrad in full pursuit now. He was yelling something that Sophia couldn't make out. When they got to the end of the drive, she backed into the street and shifted, speeding forward and pulling the car out of his reach.

As she drove, traveling as fast as possible, Sophia took several deep breaths. When she could no longer see Conrad in the rearview mirror, she noticed that her arms were shaking as she gripped the steering wheel.

She glanced over at Lorraine. "Are you okay?"

Lorraine braced herself on the car dashboard and nodded, speaking after a few moments. "Yes, I'm okay. Thank you so much for coming to get me, Dr. Strand. I don't know how I'll ever repay you."

Sophia thought about how Conrad had been hiding in the forest. "I'm glad I got to you in time. Who knows what he would have done next. Given his disturbing behavior, I really think that you were in danger." She checked the rearview mirror again but the road behind them remained void of cars. "You turned off the phone he gave you?"

Lorraine nodded. "I thought about throwing it away, but I have it in my bag. It's off, and I even took out the battery."

"Okay, good. I'm going to take you back to Orange County right now. There are two ways down the mountain. Hopefully, Conrad will take the other way. Once we get back to Orange, we'll figure out next steps."

As Sophia drove, checking frequently in her rearview mirror, she noticed that Lorraine gradually began to relax.

"I don't see anyone behind us, so I think we're safe," said Sophia. "You look exhausted. Try closing your eyes for a few minutes."

Lorraine did as Sophia suggested, laying her head on the seat. Before long, she appeared to be dozing.

As she drove, Sophia thought about what could have happened if she hadn't shown up to get Lorraine. From his forceful, erratic behavior, Conrad appeared to be a very dangerous man.

When they arrived in Orange County, Sophia drove to a hotel near her condo and stopped the car.

"We're safely in Orange," she said. "I'm going to check you into a room here, so you can get some rest. We'll reconvene in the morning."

Lorraine hugged her purse to herself. "Thank you so much, Dr. Strand. I don't know what would have happened if you didn't come to rescue me."

Sophia was about to get out of the car when she remembered something. "When he was running after the car, Conrad was yelling at us," said Sophia. "I couldn't make out what he was saying. Could you?"

"Oh, I know exactly what he was saying. He has said it to me many times."

"What does he say to you?"

"I will always find you. You will never escape me."

When Sophia got home a few minutes later, she found Teddy in the kitchen cleaning up.

"Everyone left a while ago, and Grandma went to bed." He slid a plate into the cupboard and eyed his mother for a moment. "Did everything work out with the patient?"

"It did," said Sophia, suddenly feeling a giant weight of fatigue overtake her. "Thank you for doing the dishes and for taking over as host. I'm really sorry I missed the rest of the night. I hope it was fun."

"It was a blast. Professor Kirten and Grandma entertained us all with their many adventures. Did you know they have both ridden camels in Egypt, and they both didn't like it at all?"

"That is funny," said Sophia. "I'm glad the night went well."

"You want some dessert? The pie Professor Kirten brought was really good. I saved you a slice."

"I'd love it," said Sophia, who went to the kitchen sink to wash her hands.

Teddy pulled a plate out of the oven and set it on the table with a fork. "I'd offer ice cream but we ate it all."

"I'm sure it will be great without it." Sophia took a mouthful and chewed. "Mm, you weren't kidding about it being delicious."

Teddy put two glasses of water on the island, then sat down across from her.

As he did so, Sophia felt a surge of love for her son. "You're so good to me, Teddy. Thank you."

He laughed. "It's just a piece of pie and a glass of water."

Sophia took a long drink and put the glass down. "It's much more than that, and you know it. I might not say it enough, but I feel really blessed to have you as a son."

"You say it all the time, Mom, but I'm not going to complain. The way I see it, you deserve it."

Sophia reached for a napkin. "How so?"

"It must have been tough to raise me when you were so young. I guess because I'm getting older now, I've thought about that recently. You weren't much older than I am now when I was born. I know you had help from Aunt Cathy and Uncle Chuck, but it couldn't have been easy."

"It wasn't easy. It was really rough, actually, but I don't regret even a moment of it." Sophia eyed her son's face closely. "What's got you thinking along these lines?"

"I'm not thinking about fatherhood, if that's what you're wondering. I'm definitely planning on waiting a while to be a dad. It's just..." He paused and looked over her shoulder, then back into her eyes. "I know this is probably not my place or my business, but you've been alone a long time, Mom. I'm all grown up now, and you did a good job. I know you really loved Dad and still do, but I was serious when I told you that I'd be okay with you dating. Actually, better than okay." He sat still and visibly held his breath, waiting for her response.

Sophia gave him a small smile. "You can breathe, Teddy."

He let out a big breath. "Sorry, I've been wanting to say that for a long time."

Sophia was curious. "How long?"

"I don't know, like two years now, at least."

Sophia thought through her answer for a moment. "I appreciate your concern about me and my dating life, or should I say lack of a dating life. Of course, I do still really love your father. As for dating, it's something I'm considering, okay, so no need to worry about me."

Teddy grinned. "Really? Anyone in particular?"

Sophia thought of running into Ryan earlier that day. She picked up her dishes. "No one in particular. It's just something I've been thinking about recently, too."

"Will you let me know when there is someone in particular?" asked Teddy.

Sophia took the dishes to the kitchen sink. "You'll be the first to know."

The next morning, Sophia checked her text messages to find a message from Lorraine: *I got the first good night sleep in forever last night, Dr. Strand. Thank you so much for bringing me here. I feel like a new person. Let me know what you think we should do today.*

Sophia stretched and got up to raise her blinds to reveal a bright and sunny morning. Teddy had school, and they hadn't made any plans. Sophia hoped that her grandmother would be fine with hanging around the house.

After Sophia dressed, she found her in the kitchen humming and stirring a bowl of oatmeal.

"You're in a good mood."

Her grandmother smiled widely. "I'm nearly always in a good mood."

"True," said Sophia. "But you seem especially chipper today. How was last night with Professor Kirten? I heard you were both the life of the party with your stories about far off travels. I had no idea you don't like camels."

Her grandmother opened a packet of raisins and sprinkled some on top of her oatmeal. "Smelly creatures that aren't all that nice," she said. "Yes, you were right. There, I've said it. I do enjoy Randall's company. He's a darling man. So courteous and easy to talk to."

"Well, good. Changing the subject, I need to have a session with that client today. Hopefully you can keep yourself occupied or maybe do something with Teddy when he gets back from school."

"I'll be fine," said her grandmother as she drizzled honey over her oatmeal. "Randall and I are going to a movie." Then her phone buzzed. "Excuse me, that's probably him now."

An hour later, Sophia picked Lorraine up from the hotel and took her to the counseling center, then locked the door behind them. It was Monday, and Cathy was at a one-day conference, so she wouldn't be coming in.

In her office, Sophia set her things down and turned on the fountain. "I'm glad to hear that you slept well last night. A good night's sleep always helps us reach clarity more easily. Go ahead and get comfortable on the couch. I think you will likely agree that a regression is in order. The sooner we get to the bottom of what happened between you and Conrad, the more ammunition we'll have as to how you can deal with him now."

"I'm still really worried about Stan and what he could be thinking right now, but you're right, it helps to have a good night's sleep and a clear head," she said. "A regression is definitely in order. I'm more than ready to find out what happened all those years ago." Lorraine lay back and closed her eyes as Sophia turned on the sound of light rain and started the regression.

As soon as Suzette walked through the purple door, she wanted to turn back. They were in a men's club she'd been to before with the other girls. And nothing good had ever happened here. A man played the piano and sang a Nat King Cole song, and the air hung heavy with cigarette smoke. Usually, the smell didn't bother her, but tonight her head pounded and her stomach felt awful. She had thrown up before they left the house, and she was afraid she might do so again. When she saw they were walking straight toward a group of men around a table, she felt a slithering unease.

"What the hell is wrong with you?" Vincent hissed in her ear as he marched her toward the men. "Stand up straight and smile for Christ's sake."

"I don't feel well," she said under her breath, but Vincent heard.

"I don't care if you don't feel well. Get over it. These men are paying a lot of money for tonight."

"Is anyone else coming?" asked Suzette, her stomach roiling as the men leered and cheered at her.

"I've got Rand bringing a couple more girls, but you're the main attraction now. You screw this up, you will be sorry."

Then he pushed her toward the table and said, "Gentlemen, meet Suzette. She'll be keeping you company while we round up some more party favors for the night. In the meantime, I'll get you all another round."

A bald man with a lurid grin grabbed Suzette by the hand and pulled her onto his lap as the man next to him protested. "Hey, who said you can go first."

The man ignored him and began to massage the sides of her short skirt. She could feel his arousal growing under her bottom. The noxious cocktail of alcohol and smoke, combined with the prickling of the man's hairy arms against hers unsettled Suzette's stomach so badly that she put her hand to her mouth as the nausea erupted, but she couldn't hold it back and threw up all over the table in front of him.

"What the hell!" yelled the man, pushing back his chair and throwing her off him.

Vincent apologized profusely. "I'll send someone to clean this up, and we'll make up for this, I promise."

Then he marched her out to the car and rapped on the driver's side window.

Silvester cranked down the window. "Yeah, boss?"

"Take her to Gloria and have her check her out. If she thinks she's knocked up, I want it out right away."

Silvester got out and opened the back door and waited for Suzette to get in. Then he started the car and headed away from the club.

Did she hear Vincent right? Could she be pregnant? As they made their way through the streets of Chicago, Suzette thought how it all made sense. She recalled how badly she had been feeling for a few weeks now and the overpowering urge to throw up all the time.

Silvester met her eyes in the rearview mirror. He looked like he felt sorry for her. "You okay? Let me know if you need to stop."

"Thanks, but I think I'm okay for now." She moved closer to the back window, which was partway down. The fresh air was making her feel better.

At one point, when Silvester stopped the car and waited for a man and woman to cross the street, Suzette felt a surge of envy. The couple walked arm-in-arm and were laughing. They looked so happy. She put her hands on her belly and thought about how she was supposed to be married when she got pregnant and happy and protected and loved. What kind of world would her baby be born into?

When they got to a rundown section of town, Silvester pulled the car to a halt in front of a small shop with an unlit neon sign that said pharmacy. He came around and opened the back door and waited for her to get out of the car. Then they walked to the front door of the dark store, and he knocked several times. After a few minutes, a woman opened the door. She wore a black robe over pajamas, and her hair was mussed, as if she'd been sleeping. She let them in, then shut and locked the door behind them and flipped on the overhead light. She looked at Suzette, then asked Silvester, "What's the problem?"

"She threw up. He wants her checked."

The woman led them through the store lined with shelves of medical supplies to a small back room that looked like a storage closet, except for the metal table in the center of the space. The woman, who hadn't bothered to introduce herself, gestured for Suzette to climb up on the table. Suzette complied, recoiling as the cold metal touched the back of her thighs.

The women took a small flashlight and shined it in Suzette's eyes. "You eat anything different lately, or hit your head hard?"

Suzette shook her head. "No."

"How long has the throwing up been going on?"

"Two or three weeks."

"When was the last time you had your cycle?"

"It's been a little more than a month."

"Do you have headaches? And do certain smells make you want to vomit more than others?"

"Yes, a lot of headaches, and certain things do make me want to throw up more than others."

The woman sighed and turned to Silvester. "She's probably pregnant. I could give her a physical exam, but it's too soon for me to see or feel anything. I know Vincent doesn't like to wait for test results. The quickest option is for me to do a dilation and curettage like I did with the last one. That'll take care of the problem. She'll be good to work in a couple of days."

"Okay, go ahead. I'll wait in the car."

The woman yawned and opened a cupboard, pulling out a cloth gown and handing it to Suzette. "I'm going to get dressed. In the meantime, take off your clothes and put this on."

After the woman left, Suzette was seized with terror. Just like that, this woman was going to kill her baby because Vincent ordered it? She saw a door at the back of the room marked exit and ran over to it. After removing her heels, she unlatched the door and pushed it open, the chilly night air rushing at her. She slipped out into a back alley and closed the door quietly behind her. Then she started running.

Chapter 20

Lorraine had been under for some time. When she began to look like she was straining against something, her breathing becoming labored, Sophia decided to bring her back.

"I'm going to have you return to Orange now, Lorraine," she said. "Look for the purple door and begin walking toward it. I'm going to begin counting backward from twenty. When we reach one, you will turn the doorknob and walk back into the present here in Orange, California. Twenty, nineteen, slowly walk toward the purple door, eighteen, seventeen, sixteen, you are getting closer to coming back to the now, fifteen, fourteen, thirteen, twelve, getting ever nearer, eleven, ten, nine, eight, you are just about there, seven, six, five, four, get ready to open the door, three, two, one. You can open your eyes. You are now safely back in Orange."

Sophia waited for Lorraine to open her eyes. At this point in the regressions, she always felt some trepidation that the person might not come out of the meditation or return in an altered state. But to her relief, Lorraine's eyelids soon fluttered open, and she turned to look at Sophia.

"I know what happened back then," she said. "Not all of it, because you brought me back before I could see how it ended. But I was pregnant in that lifetime, and Vincent wanted the baby aborted."

"Wanted?"

"Right before you brought me back, I ran out the back door of this pharmacy where a woman was about to do the procedure."

"Do you know where you were going?"

Lorraine closed her eyes. "I can see myself running down a dark alley, and I was barefoot. I think it's the same vision I had when I cut my foot. I could hear cars driving and occasional honking, and voices. But I don't know where I was going. Maybe I didn't even know. I just remember being terrified about her killing my baby." Her hands went to her abdomen. "Just like in this lifetime, I knew that I wanted the baby, and I would do anything to save him."

"Well, the good news is that we live in a much different time today. It will be a lot easier for you to keep your baby. And there are protections for women that weren't in place in the 1940s."

"You mean from domestic abuse and stalking?"

"Yes, and that being said, I think it's time for you to get a restraining order against Conrad. I also think that it would be a good idea to come clean with Stan. I can arrange a meeting with all of us if you want."

Lorraine gazed at the fountain for a few moments, then replied, "I think you're right. I know enough now about what happened to explain things to Stan. And to be honest, I don't think I want to know what ended up happening to me and my baby in that other lifetime. Maybe what I know is enough. And you're right about Conrad. It's time I stood up to his stalking. The sooner I do that the better."

She motioned to stand up but sat back down.

"Are you feeling lightheaded?" asked Sophia.

"Yes, it could be because I haven't eaten since last night. I keep forgetting that I'm eating for two."

Sophia checked her phone. "Tell you what. I'll go get you something to eat. Why don't you rest while I'm gone. My colleague isn't coming in today, so it will be nice and quiet."

Lorraine considered. "Okay, thank you, Dr. Strand. That sounds like a good idea."

When Sophia returned a few minutes later, she found Lorraine fast asleep. She set their lunches down on her desk and quietly ate the chicken rice bowl she had gotten herself, all the while wondering how this whole mess could ever be rectified. She had offered to have a session with Lorraine and Stan, but what if the baby wasn't his? And what about Conrad? He seemed increasingly unstable, and that very much concerned her.

Lorraine was just starting to wake up when Sophia heard a loud rapping at the front door.

"Who is that? Do you think it's Conrad?" she asked.

Sophia pulled open her laptop. "Let me check the security camera." Sure enough, a man looking like the one she'd seen chasing their car the night before was pounding on the front door.

Lorraine came to look over her shoulder and gasped. "That's Conrad. What do we do?"

Sophia reached for her phone. "I'm calling the police."

It wasn't long before sirens sounded in the parking lot and car doors opened.

"They're here, but you're going to need to go out there with me," said Sophia. "I can corroborate your story, but they're going to need to hear it from you how Conrad has been following you and threatening you."

Lorraine looked panicked, but she nodded and followed Sophia out to the front of the building. When Sophia unlocked the door and stepped outside, two police officers were questioning Conrad. He immediately saw Lorraine behind her and cried out, "There you are, Lorraine! I was just explaining how I came to find you because I was so worried. I'm sorry if I alarmed anyone with my knocking. I thought you might not be able to hear me."

One of the police officers, a lanky man with wire-rim glasses, turned to Sophia and Lorraine and asked, "Do you know this man?"

"My name is Dr. Sophia Strand, and this is my office. I am the one who called 911. I do not know this man, but I know of him. He is associated with my client, Lorraine Donovan. It has been my observation during my treatment of Lorraine that this man has displayed obsessive tendencies, including stalking her. In fact, he ran after our car last night when I went to pick her up in Lake Arrowhead."

Conrad started to protest, but the officer put up a hand to stop him. "You can tell your side of the story in a minute."

He turned to Lorraine. "Is what Dr. Strand is saying correct? Has this man been harassing you?"

Lorraine glanced at Conrad, then looked at the ground.

"Just tell the truth, Lorraine," said Sophia.

She raised her head and nodded. "Everything Dr. Strand said is correct. Conrad has been following me and calling me over and over, even though I've told him I don't want to talk to him."

The officer turned to Conrad now. "Is what she is saying correct? Have you been following her?"

"Yes, but I was just concerned about her. I wanted to make sure she was okay. Let's talk this out like adults, Lorraine. No need to involve the police."

Lorraine stood up straighter now and looked Conrad in the eye. "The police are already involved, and they need to be. I want you to leave me alone. To ensure that you do, I'm going to file a restraining order against you."

When she mentioned the restraining order, Conrad, who until that moment had been holding it together, exploded. "A restraining order? What a bunch of crap. You're all over me, and now you want a restraining order." He started to advance toward Lorraine, but the officer pulled him back.

"We're bringing you into the station until you can cool off," he told him. Then he turned to Lorraine. "I'd advise you to come in as well, to file the restraining order."

As they took Conrad away, Sophia could see Lorraine visibly shaking. "I can go with you to the station, if you want."

Lorraine squared her shoulders. "Thank you, Dr. Strand, but just give me a ride there. You've already done too much. I need to face this myself. And then I need to talk to Stan."

Chapter 21

"How was the movie?" Sophia asked her grandmother when she returned to the condo after dropping Lorraine at the police station.

"The movie could have been better, but the company and popcorn were wonderful." Her grandmother was sitting in the living room with a cup of tea. "Come tell me how it's going with your client."

Sophia sat down next to her grandmother and sighed. "We've made some strides, but I'm concerned that I'm not doing this right."

Her grandmother chuckled. "There is no right, as you're likely finding, but I'm happy to weigh in if you want to give me the basics."

Sophia decided to take her up on the offer and gave her a brief overview of the day's occurrences.

"I think the idea to speak to her and her husband together is a good one, but I feel that she needs to complete the regression before you do so. Without the end to that story, it will be difficult, if not impossible, for them to know where to go from here."

"She is hesitant about finding out what occurred all those years ago, and I can't blame her. It could end up being a very traumatic outcome. I am really wondering if it would cause more harm than good to dig up the past with all its skeletons. I'm also concerned about my culpability in all of this by facilitating her digging up that past."

"You didn't dig up the past, that's impossible," said her grandmother. "The past came back to confront your client when that man walked into her life. You've been helping her see her way more clearly, that's all."

"What do I do about completing the regression so she can see everything clearly, then? As far as I know, she may be talking to her husband right now."

"It'll all work out. You'll see." Her grandmother stood and picked up her teacup. "I've got to get ready."

"Get ready for what?"

"Randall is taking me out for dinner."

Sophia gave her a surprised look. "What if I had made plans for us?"

"You didn't, and you'll be busy tonight, anyway."

Later that night when the house was quiet, Sophia set down the book she'd been reading and decided to take a bath. It looked like her grandmother's prediction that she would be busy wasn't going to come true, so she might as well get a good soak in and go to bed early. Just as she was walking down the hall, her phone began ringing. She went to retrieve it from the kitchen counter and checked the screen. Lorraine's number. "Hello?"

"Dr. Strand, I am so sorry to bother you again, but it's all such a mess."

Sophia leaned against the counter. "What is all such a mess?"

"The police didn't grant the restraining order, after all."

"Why not?"

"It came out that Conrad and I were lovers, and he said that even though I was a married woman, I wouldn't stay away from him. But that's not the worst of it. Stan showed up at the police station. He saw Conrad and me, and then all hell broke loose."

"How did he end up coming to the police station?"

"Conrad had called a work colleague, but the colleague wasn't available, so he called Stan for help. When Stan walked in and saw us both, it was as if he knew. He exploded and took a run at Conrad, but the police stopped him and told him to leave, or they'd lock him up."

"Where are you now?"

"I'm standing in front of your office. I took an Uber here."

"I'll be right there."

When Sophia arrived a few minutes later, she checked the parking lot for signs of Conrad, then ushered Lorraine inside and locked the door. Once in her office, she motioned for Lorraine to sit down and did the same. "I know you're afraid to find out what happened all those years ago with your baby, but I think the only way to any resolution for you is to finish the regression."

Lorraine sighed. "I know you're right. I might not want to know the truth, but I feel that I need to know it."

A few minutes later when Sophia had Lorraine under and led her to the purple door, she watched the woman's face intently as she began to breathe heavily.

Suzette raced down the sidewalk, aware that people were gawking at her in her short skirt and tight-fitting shirt. She had run for some minutes, her foot bleeding, when she simply couldn't go any further, so she stopped in the doorway of a closed shop to catch her breath. She might not have anywhere to go, but she knew that she had to get away from Vincent and that woman. As she stood there, she searched her mind for who might help her. It was then she thought of Officer Pete. Maybe he could help. She backtracked to a phone booth she'd seen while running and went inside to make a reverse call to him at the police station, praying he was on duty. To her relief, the operator said he was available, and he soon answered the phone.

"This is Officer Stearns."

"Officer Pete, is that you?"

"This is he. Who is calling?"

"Suzette, I mean, Evelyn. You took me into the station a few weeks ago. I was at Vincent's place."

"I remember. Are you in trouble?"

"Yes, Vincent and this woman who wants to kill my baby are after me."

"Give me your location, and I'll be right there."

When the squad car pulled up a few minutes later and Officer Pete got out and approached her, Suzette felt such relief that she ran toward him, tripping on the sidewalk and sprawling to the ground and hitting her head, then everything went black.

When she woke up, she was in the hospital, and Officer Pete was standing by the bed. "How are you feeling?" he asked.

"My head hurts. Is my baby okay?"

"Your baby is fine," he said. "The nurse heard a heartbeat."

Suzette lay back, relieved. "Thank you so much. I don't know how I'll ever repay you."

Officer Pete pulled a chair next to the bed and sat down. "I have a way for you to repay me. I'd like you to tell me all about Vincent and his operation. What he makes you and the other girls do, and who he meets with, as well as his clients. Can you do that?"

"I want to, but he said he'd kill me if I ever talked."

Officer Pete put a hand on hers. "You'll be protected, I promise. It's important we get this guy off the street. We can with your help."

Suzette thought about all the times that Vincent had hurt her and the other girls, and how he had wanted to kill her baby. "I'll do it," she said finally.

At that moment, time shifted, and Suzette found herself in a nursery. In a crib lay a baby boy, his plump cheeks rosy, his eyes closed. She sensed someone behind her, then strong, solid arms embraced her. "Your baby and you are beautiful," said Pete in her ear.

At one point, Sophia noticed that it almost looked like Lorraine had fallen asleep. She let her stay in the transitive state for some time before bringing her out. When she did so, Lorraine's eyes opened, and she slowly sat up on the couch.

Chapter 22

"What did you see during your regression?" asked Sophia.

Lorraine told her about how she had gone to court and testified against Vincent, along with some of the other girls, and how he was put behind bars for many years because of their testimony.

"Pete, or should I say, Stan, accepted me and the baby, even though the baby wasn't his. I'm guessing at that time determining paternity wasn't something you could easily do, so I must have never known if the baby was Vincent's or Pete's." She was thoughtful for a moment, then asked, "Were you serious about seeing Stan and me together so that I can explain all of this?"

Sophia nodded.

"I know it's so late, but could I call him right now and see if he'll come in? He was so upset at the station, he might not answer, but it's worth a try."

Sophia glanced at the clock on the wall to see that it was midnight. "Go ahead."

When he answered, Lorraine said quickly, "Stan, baby, please don't hang up. Hear me out. I'm at my therapist's office, and I really want to explain things to you. Could you come here?"

To Sophia's surprise, Stan agreed.

Twenty minutes later, Sophia went to the door and opened it.

"You must be Stan," she said as she let him in. "I'm Dr. Sophia Strand."

"Nice to meet you," he said, shaking her hand. He was tall and wiry, with close-set eyes and short brown hair.

"Lorraine is in my office. Follow me."

When they entered the room, Lorraine sprung up from the couch. "Stan, I'm so glad you agreed to come."

He looked from her to Sophia, then cleared his throat. "Where would you like me to sit?"

"You may sit next to your wife, if you wish, or we can pull the chair at my desk over," said Sophia.

Stan stood there for a moment, then walked over to the couch and waited for his wife to sit before sitting down next to her.

Sophia sat in her armchair across from them. "As Lorraine mentioned, I'm your wife's therapist. I am a licensed clinical psychologist. I'm also a past life regression therapist, which factors in here."

At the mention of past life regression, Stan looked surprised. "Okay, I'm listening."

"Lorraine came to me through a referral from her sister, Dahlia. She wanted to understand why she had become entangled with Conrad in this lifetime. How she'd ended up under his spell and had acted in ways that are uncharacteristic."

"Remember how Kevin and Dahlia were having all that trouble with her ex-husband? That was because she'd known him in a past life," explained Lorraine.

Stan stared at the floor for a moment and sighed. "I can't believe I'm about to ask this, but are you trying to tell me you've known Conrad in a past life?"

Lorraine nodded. "Yes, he was my..." She didn't finish the sentence.

"Stan, generally when people are introduced to this subject, there is quite a bit of explanation prior. In your wife's case, she wanted to reach out to you as soon as possible to explain, because of what occurred in the police station earlier."

Stan ran his hands through his hair. "This subject isn't entirely new to me. My mother believed in past lives."

Lorraine looked shocked. "I didn't know that."

"It isn't exactly conversation material, and for many years I thought she was crazy, but there were a lot of things that made sense in later years. Especially after she died."

"Lorraine, why don't you fill Stan in as to what has occurred with Conrad in this and the past lifetime."

As Lorraine explained what had transpired with Conrad over the last year, Stan's face at first showing no emotion, became stormy when she described how he had tricked her into going on dates with other men and then had used those actions against her.

When she finished, Stan said, "So, you're saying I was a police officer in my past life?" He shook his head. "That would explain my preoccupation with wanting to be a cop when I was young. My father talked me out of it and insisted I go to law school."

"Do you have any questions for Lorraine after hearing all of this?" asked Sophia.

Stan looked at Lorraine for the first time since he had sat down next to her. "Yes, just one. Do you love Conrad?"

"Oh, god, no! I love you, Stan. And I always will, even if you can't forgive me, which I would understand."

He looked at Sophia. "From your professional opinion, can we get past this?"

"If you're asking if you can both work this out between the two of you, I think that's possible. I'll be happy to counsel you through it. Now that the regression therapy is complete, Conrad no longer has a hold on Lorraine. But there is one matter that Lorraine hasn't mentioned that is very important."

Eyes bright, Lorraine said, "I'm pregnant."

At the stunned look on Stan's face, she added, "And I'm not sure if the baby is yours or Conrad's, but I'm going to have a test and find out."

Stan stared at the floor for a few long moments before replying. "When can you get the test?"

"Next week," said Lorraine.

Stan reached out and took her hand. "It's late. Let's go home. We'll deal with the truth when we have it."

When Sophia got home that night, all was quiet and the lights were off. As she got ready for bed, she thought about Lorraine and Stan walking out of her office hand-in-hand and the enduring nature of love. She fell into bed utterly exhausted. Just as she was drifting off, she heard Phillip whisper in her ear, "Well done, my love."

Chapter 23

Sophia took the next few days off to spend time with her grandmother and Teddy when he could join them. Professor Kirten also came along for some outings. In fact, he was around quite a bit in the following days, and it delighted Sophia to see how well he and her grandmother got along. He would rush to open doors for her and often brought her and Sophia flowers. Grandmother even beat him at chess, which Sophia secretly suspected he'd let her do, but he wasn't talking.

On her grandmother's last night, they all went out to one of Sophia's favorite restaurants in the Orange Plaza, Citrus City Grille. Though the November evening was brisk, they decided to sit out on the patio.

"It's good for the digestion to eat outdoors when the weather is nippy," announced Professor Kirten as he pulled out chairs for Sophia, her grandmother, and Cerise. Once they were seated and began examining the drink menu, Professor Kirten waved to someone walking along the sidewalk and called out, "Ryan, my boy, so nice to see you!"

Sophia looked up to see the man she'd met at the grocery store the other day. He stopped on the sidewalk next to where they sat and gave them an easy smile. "Randall, so nice to see you."

"Everyone, meet one of my esteemed colleagues at the university, Professor Ryan Collins. And allow me to introduce you to my friends

Sophia, her grandmother Ophelia, her son Teddy, and his companion Cerise."

Ryan turned to Sophia, his eyes twinkling, and said, "Sophia and I met the other day over breadcrumbs. Very nice to see you again."

Trying hard not to blush, Sophia fumbled for her voice, finally replying, "Very nice to see you again, Ryan."

"Won't you join us?" asked her grandmother.

"I'm on my way to have dinner with my brother and his wife, so I will regretfully have to pass. But thank you so much for the invitation. Maybe another time?"

"We'll hold you to that," said Professor Kirten.

"I'll let you get back to your dinner," said Ryan, who before walking off, gave them all another big smile, and was that a quick wink directed at Sophia?

After she watched him walk away and turned back to her menu, she almost burst out laughing at the grins on everyone's faces.

It was Teddy who spoke up first. "You holding out on us, Mom? I thought we had an agreement."

"What are you talking about?" said Sophia. "Like Ryan said, we met at the grocery store the other day. I don't know anything about him. He could be married, for all I know."

"Oh, he's not married," said Professor Kirten. "He's very single."

Teddy's eyebrows lifted. "Did you hear that, Mom. He's very single."

"I'm not hard of hearing Teddy. And what does very single mean, anyway?"

"I think it means that there's absolutely, positively no woman he's involved with in his life," offered Cerise.

At that, the whole table began to laugh, including Cerise.

The next morning when Sophia dropped her grandmother off at the airport, they hugged, and the older woman took Sophia's hands in hers. "What an absolutely lovely trip I've had, little love. So many wonderful memories."

"I'm so glad to hear that," said Sophia. "I was worried about my absences because of work, but then you and Teddy and Professor Kirten had each other's company. Did I hear right? He's visiting you in Greece?"

"Yes, Randall has already bought the airline tickets. He'll be coming in January before he begins teaching his new class. I like that about him. That he continues to work like me. Most men I've met my age are content to sit and stare at the sea or worse the television set."

Sophia squeezed her grandmother's hands. "I'm so happy that I insisted on you meeting each other."

"And what of that man we met last night, Randall's colleague, Ryan?"

"What of him?"

Her grandmother smiled. "You like him. I could see it on your face, and he is obviously enamored with you."

"I don't know about that, grandmother," she said. "But if he happens to reach out, I'll be amenable."

"Oh, he'll reach out," said her grandmother. Then she pecked her granddaughter on both cheeks and wheeled her carryon through security, turning once to blow her a kiss.

As Sophia made her way out of the airport, she thought about how she usually felt so melancholy when her grandmother left, but this time she felt better about it. Maybe because she knew Professor Kirten would be going to see her soon, and she wouldn't be alone. As she walked to her car, she thought about how learning to enjoy being alone was a good thing, and even advised at times, but it could begin to wear away at you over time.

Just as she reached her car, her cellphone rang. She stopped to pull it out of her purse. It was Lorraine.

Chapter 24

"I'm so glad I got you on the phone, Dr. Strand." Lorraine sounded upbeat. "I'm not bothering you, am I? Do you have a moment?"

Sophia opened her car door and slid inside. "Not at all. It sounds like you might have good news to report?"

"Oh, Dr. Strand, the absolute best! First of all, Stan has agreed to give me another chance. He'd like me to set up some sessions for us with you. To talk through what happened and how we can make our marriage stronger. Second, and probably the best news of all, I got the paternity test. The baby is Stan's, and it's a boy!"

"I'm so happy for you," said Sophia.

"I think Stan would have raised the baby, even if it wasn't his, but this makes things so much easier."

"Not to spoil the mood, but any news on Conrad?"

"That's right, more good news. Stan looked into Conrad's actions, and it turns out that he has been displaying questionable behavior for a while, including with other wives, so I wasn't the only one. We've reported him, and the authorities are looking into him for running an illegal escort service."

"That is good news," said Sophia. "I'll get back to you regarding setting up some appointments. You take care of yourself and that baby."

Lorraine laughed. "No danger of me not doing that. Stan is making sure of it." She paused, and Sophia sensed she had teared up. "Thank you again, Dr. Strand. If I hadn't gotten your help with this, I'm sure my marriage would have ended, and I hate to think about it, but I don't know what would have happened to my baby. Conrad is a dangerous man. I can see that clearly now. I'm going to tell everyone I know about how much you helped me. The least I can do is get you some new clients."

"I appreciate that Lorraine. You take care now."

She put away her phone, and as she started to turn on the car engine, glanced in the rearview mirror and gasped. "It would be nice if you could give a warning before you do that," she said to Phillip's reflection.

"Sorry, love, but you were busy talking. I just wanted to congratulate you on a job well done. I knew you could do it."

Sophia smiled. "Thank you. I have a feeling I had some help from you."

"Perhaps," said Phillip. "I also wanted to tell you that it's okay with me, actually more than okay with me, if when Ryan calls to ask you out for coffee that you go."

"How did?" Sophia started to ask, then shook her head. "Of course, you were there."

"Ryan is a great guy. He's had his own share of heartache, but I'll let him tell you about it."

"What kind of heartache?" she asked. But Phillip had vanished.

Lorraine proved true to her word regarding getting Sophia business. Within two weeks, she had three new past life clients, including the one she was currently waiting for. At exactly three in the afternoon, a woman appeared at the front door of the center and pushed it open. She was of average height and wore a grim expression that matched the dark pants and gray blouse she wore. Marching up to Sophia with an outstretched hand, she announced, "I am Lenka. You are Dr. Strand?"

Sophia took her hand, and they shook. "Yes, I am. Very nice to meet you, Lenka."

In her office, Sophia indicated for Lenka to sit across from her desk. The woman did so, perching on the edge of the chair, her back ramrod straight.

"How do you know Lorraine?" asked Sophia.

"She is my neighbor and speaks very highly of you and what you do. As I mentioned on the phone, she told me about her past life experience, and I believe my current circumstance also started in a past life. To give you some background, I am originally from Slovakia. I emigrated here ten years ago. My uncle has lived here for thirty years. He sponsored me and my son."

Sophia nodded for her to go on.

"At first, I thought that maybe the dream I have been having for a couple of years now was related to my being a foreigner in a strange land. My uncle has done what he can to help me adjust in the United States, including finding me a job, but I've found that adjusting is a long process."

"I imagine it is," said Sophia.

"As I said, I've been having the dream for some time. Then a couple of months ago, the dream began to interfere with my waking hours, coming to me when I'm at work and driving and things like that. It has become very disruptive." She stopped and cleared her throat.

"So, you're now having visions while awake, as well as the dreams?"

"Yes, and it's always the same vision, whether I'm awake or asleep. I'm walking down a road, and there are many people walking with me. It's as if we are being herded like cattle. There is a man on horseback who rides back and forth and snaps his whip at those who begin to fall behind. I'm traveling with a young child, a boy, who I think is my son. I'm pulling him along, but he is stumbling. Though we are walking with a group, I sense I am alone with my son. The others walking with me appear to be strangers to me. At one point, and this is always the point where the vision or dream ends, my son falls and hurts himself and begins crying. I try to quiet him by picking him up and continuing to walk with him, but he won't stop wailing. Then, the man on horseback begins riding next to us and shouts in Russian, "Shut him up, or he will die.""

When Lenka stopped talking, silence filled the room for a moment. After it became apparent that she didn't have anything else to say, Sophia said, "That is a disturbing story."

Lenka sat up straighter. "That's just it, Dr. Strand, I don't think it's a story." She put her hand on her chest. "I feel in my heart that what I'm seeing has happened to me in a prior lifetime. And I believe that my son did die at the hands of the man on horseback."

Sophia uncrossed her legs and moved forward slightly. "Apart from this horrible vision, how is this affecting your current lifetime?"

"I am a single mother, and I have a son in this lifetime. His father died before we came here. Recently, my son was diagnosed with leukemia. The doctors say there is reason to have hope in terms of his prognosis, but I feel deep in my soul that we are about to repeat a pattern. And I have no idea how to stop it."

Read Lenka's story in *Suspended Exodus*, coming soon!

A Note For You

Dear Reading Gem,

Thanks for spending time with me and Sophia!

Past lives collide with current lifetimes in The Past Life Prism Series. Starring Sophia Strand, a past life regression therapist, the series chronicles the torrid tales of significant relationships spanning centuries. Watch romance kindled, sparks fly, and intrigue unveiled as couples reunite in present day.

If you like the series, please leave a review or just stars on any book review platform. Your opinion matters and is incredibly powerful.

Thanks again and talk soon!

Stay Enlightened

Thanks for reading! Let's stay in touch. I post insider information, and sneak peeks of upcoming books on my website at https://www.juliebaw dendavis.com/fiction. You can also email me at Julie@JulieBawden Davis.com, find me on Facebook, and follow me on Amazon.

Even better, join my weekly VIP Reading Gems newsletter here. When signing up, you get a free copy of *Discovered Beginnings*, the prequel novella to my Discovered Truth Series. There are also lots of giveaways and contests!

Escape to Unforgettable Romance and Intrigue...

Books by Julie Bawden-Davis

The Past Life Prism Series
(Romantic Time Travel Suspense)
Suspended: The Beginning
Suspended Enforcement
Suspended Entrapment
Suspended Exodus
Suspended Entanglement

The Discovered Truth Series
(Romantic Suspense)
Discovered Beginnings:
(FREE at https://www.juliebawdendavis.com/fiction)
Discovered Secrets
Discovered Memories
Discovered Indiscretions
Discovered Liaisons
Discovered Betrayal
Discovered Denial
Discovered Distractions
Discovered Deception
Discovered Lies

Discovered Vengeance
Discovered Redemption
Discovered Obsession
Discovered Transgressions
Discovered Suspicion
Discovered Escape
Discovered Promises
Discovered Cover-Up
Discovered Intentions